USBORNE
Forgotten Fairy Tales
of
Kindness
and COURAGE

Retold by Mary Sebag-Montefiore
with a foreword by Dr. Zoe Williams

Illustrated by Josy Bloggs, Maribel Lechuga,
Maxine Lee-Mackie and Khoa Le

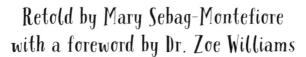

Contents

Forgotten Fairy Tales of Kindness and COURAGE

Foreword

Books and stories have the power to entertain, help our brains develop and inspire our imagination. But the stories in this book do much more than that. Each of these vividly exciting and wildly adventurous tales has a life lesson or two to teach as well.

I still distinctly remember many of the wisdoms that I have acquired from childhood stories. *The Hare and the Tortoise* and *The Boy Who Cried Wolf*, to name just a couple, taught me

important lessons on which I have based many an important decision. To think that the stories in this beautiful book could have been lost to history! What a tragedy that would have been. Though the original tales are over 100 years old, the teachings that they convey are as apt today as they ever have been.

I especially love how these stories show us that there are many ways to be brave. It takes courage to fight off a goblin, but it's also important to see characters who have the courage to stand up for themselves, stand up for others and to stand up for what is right.

Both girls and boys can be heroes and the beautiful illustrations show us a diverse range of genders and ethnicities in the characters in the stories – something that is not widespread even today and very much welcomed…

Stories create a place for us to lose ourselves in our imagination, venture to another world and transform ourselves, for a short while, into another being. In fact one of the stories, which is aptly named *The Girl in the Book*, tells the tale of exactly that.

Ultimately these stories help us understand and value the importance of kindness for ourselves, compassion for others and the courage to be brave and stand up for what is right.

I cannot think of anything more important.

And wouldn't the world be a brighter place if we all had a little more kindness and courage?

Dr. Zoe Williams

NHS doctor and TV presenter

This story is based on a
book by Dinah Craik, first
published in 1874.

The Prince
in the Tower

Prince Henry was the most beautiful baby prince ever born. At least, that's what his parents, the King and Queen, thought. The only person who wasn't pleased about the Prince was the King's brother. He'd been getting excited about being King himself, if no heir ever came along.

But the King made his brother a duke to make him feel better, and gave a great big party for the new little Prince's naming ceremony. The Queen organized new clothes and feasting for everyone in the kingdom, even though she felt very ill. She couldn't go to the party, but lay in bed.

Prince Henry's nanny was very kind, but not very elegant, so a fashionable young lady was chosen to hold the baby during the procession through the crowds. She wasn't used to holding babies, and she dropped him on the marble stairs before they started. No one saw, except one little old woman, who seemed to pop up from nowhere, and whispered, "I am the baby's Godmother. Don't drop him again!"

"Get out of my way, crone," said the elegant lady, but she spoke to the air, for the old woman had vanished.

Shortly after the naming ceremony, the great bell in the palace, which had so recently pealed for joy, began to toll in mourning. The Queen, growing weaker and weaker, had died.

After that, the care of the baby Prince was given over entirely to his nanny. He was the happiest baby, with shining curls, but although he grew bigger, and stronger, and crowed with laughter every morning, his legs didn't seem to work. Whenever his nanny tried to help him stand, he fell straight down again.

"I don't think he'll ever walk," his nanny told the King.

And the King listened, and watched his son, and saw what the nanny said was true. But the King was very busy, running the kingdom, and wasn't able to spend as much time with the Prince as he would have liked. When the King *did* see his son, he just patted him on the head and said what a fine king he would make one day.

"But if anything should ever happen to me,"

the King said to his brother, the Duke, "will you take care of my boy?"

"Certainly," promised the Duke.

Now, soon after that, the King did die. Suddenly, Prince Henry had no one except his uncle – the Duke – and his nanny.

With all the Council and Courtiers watching, the Duke picked Henry up, sat him on the throne, and put the crown on his head. Prince Henry smiled, and that made the Council and Courtiers smile. He laughed, and that made the Council and Courtiers laugh. But then the little Prince threw his crown on the floor and began sucking his thumb. He was only a toddler, after all.

"This," said the Duke, "is your King. Do you wish to be ruled by a toddler?" he asked, with a sneer. "I will govern the country until he is older. Does anyone have any objection?"

No one did. Everyone said how lucky the Prince was to have his uncle taking care of him. The Duke brought his wife and sons to live at the Palace. Everyone saw the boys, playing in the Palace gardens, but no one ever saw Prince Henry.

"He's ill," said the Duke, to anyone who asked.

Then came the news that, for the sake of his health, Prince Henry was going away, beyond the Faraway Mountains.

He was taken with his nanny to a place that no one ever went to, or even knew about. It was a barren spot: no trees, no flowers or grass, no birds, no animals. In fact, no living things at all, just miles and miles of flat, stony sand, like a desert. In the middle of it was a round, tall tower. It had no doors and no stairs. But right at the top of the tower were four rooms, with little windows in the walls to let in the light, and inside those rooms were all the books and toys that anyone could want.

A soldier took Henry and his nanny there in a carriage. He hooked a huge ladder to the top of the tower, and helped them inside. He climbed up again with a big parcel of food, then unhooked the ladder and galloped away.

Every month, the soldier returned, bringing more food, and more books and toys. But the soldier never spoke. He'd been sworn to secrecy. If he'd brought news of the outside world, or told anyone about the Prince in the tower, he would have been thrown into prison and left there.

All too soon, people forgot about the little Prince. It was exactly what his uncle, the Duke, had intended. All the Duke had ever really wanted was to be King. He felt that what he wanted, he ought to have, and he always got his way, because people like that very often do.

Eventually, the Duke put out the news that the little Prince had died. Everyone remembered him again, and was very sorry. But because the Duke had been so cunning, no one knew the truth – that the rightful King was very much alive… far away in the secret tower.

And there Henry lived, with his nanny, in the four rooms at the top of the tall tower. He had love, for his nanny loved him just as a mother would. He had toys to play with and books to look at. He had adventures, through the pages of his books and on flights of his own imagination. But was it enough? For a growing child, filled with curiosity and energy and longing… of course it wasn't enough.

When Henry felt sad, he would pull himself

up onto the windowsill. And from there he could watch the raging storms, the shadows of the clouds and the setting sun.

Henry didn't remember the palace, but he knew he was a prince, because his nanny always told him he was one, and that he shouldn't ever forget it.

As he grew older, she taught him to read, and the longing within him only grew. For the books told him about places very different from his tower.

The Prince read at the kitchen table, where the light spilled in from the windows. He read the books hungrily, like a starving person, but it was like reading about delicious food that you know you'll never get to eat. "If only I could see it all for myself," he cried. "Oh, how I *long* to get out of here!" And at last his unhappiness welled up inside him, and burst out in a cascade of tears.

As he wept, he heard the *tap, tap, tap* of a stick. Turning around, he saw an old lady dressed in long flowing robes, with a crackle of something in the air around her, like a dark sky before a thunderstorm.

"My boy," she said. "I couldn't come until you called for me. I am your Godmother, and I'm going to help you."

"Can you get me out of here?" begged Henry.

"I don't have the power to free you," she said. "But I do have a present for you – a cloak that will take you outside and show you everything you've ever wanted to see."

"But I can't walk," explained Henry. "And I'm stuck inside this tower."

"That's why you need my present," said his Godmother, and she handed him a shabby bundle that looked like a rolled up piece of rag.

"Thank you, but… it looks a little old," said Henry, trying not to sound ungrateful.

"Old?" said his Godmother, smiling. "Maybe.

But don't let that deceive you. It's also *magic*."

"A magic cloak!" said Henry, his eyes aglow. And when he looked at his Godmother again, he saw that she was more fairy than human, with her wise and shining eyes. The crackle in the air around her wasn't electricity, he realized, but pure magic.

"Now, let me tell you how the cloak works," said his Godmother. "Open the window, then spread the cloak out on the floor and sit in the middle, like a frog on a water-lily leaf. Say *Abracadabra, dum di dum*, and see what happens. When you want to come back, just say, *Abracadabra, tum ti tum*."

And then, like a soft cloud melting into the sky, she was gone.

At that moment, Henry's nanny came into the kitchen. She hadn't heard a word of the conversation, because his Godmother had magicked it into silence.

"I'm going into my room to do some sewing. Will you be happy on your own?" she asked.

"Very happy," said Henry.

Here was his chance… The moment his nanny left and shut the door, he sprang up to the windowsill and opened the window. Then, carefully, he spread his cloak on the floor and sat in the middle, just as his Godmother had described, his heart beating fast.

"*Abracadabra, dum di dum,*" he said, laughing a little because the words sounded so silly.

The cloak rose, with Henry sitting on it. Out he flew, beyond the window, into the clear fresh air.

"Oh!" he cried. Henry had never felt such a delicious sensation as that soft air, brushing against his cheek and ruffling his hair.

On Henry flew, over barren desert, over rivers and mountains. It all looked so beautiful, especially as the sun went down and the stars came out.

But then some mist blotted out the stars and it began to rain, soaking his clothes, wetting his curls so they hung, slick and damp against his face.

"I'll have to go back," Henry thought. "Now, what are the words?" He began to panic, not knowing what to do, alone up there in the dark sky. "Godmother?" he called. "Are you there? I've forgotten the words to get home!" Instantly the words *Abracadabra, tum ti tum* tumbled into his brain.

"Thank you," he called, into the damp night air. "I'll never forget again!"

He repeated the charm and the cloak turned gently around and brought him back to the tower.

After that, Henry went away whenever he could. Soon, he was exploring further and further, in every direction, seeing all sorts of wonderful things.

He listened to the flowing of the river, the rustling of trees and the sighing of the wind. He swooped down low, mesmerized by a single blade of grass, glinting in the sunlight; by a caterpillar creeping along the ground; by insects shining red, gold, purple, blue, buzzing from flower to flower.

He learned to fly higher and higher, right to the tops of the mountains, so the world below him seemed very far away, the people just tiny dots in the landscape, like ants crawling over the hills.

He learned to fly as fast as the wind, riding the gusts like waves in the sea, his hands gripping the sides of the magical cloak. Sometimes he was followed by flocks of birds, riding the wind with him – swifts that arced and curled around him on their scythe-like wings; skeins of geese, flying together, calling in greeting, as if they were all of a kind, joined together in a fellowship of the air.

While Henry flew far and wide on his magical cloak, his Godmother gathered up handfuls of moonshine and made an image of him, so whenever his nanny peeked in to see him, she saw the image and was reassured that he was happy and well.

But however magical the cloak, there were times when Prince Henry felt nothing but sadness. He would look down and see children, playing together, and he would long to join them. "I want friends my own age," he thought. "I want to be *with* people. I want to take my part in the world."

When he thought this, he would lie on the cloak and close his eyes, letting the wind rock him gently, willing the wave of sadness to pass.

One day, as Prince Henry flew above a summer field, golden with barley, he heard a delicious sound soaring in the air. It was the song of a skylark. The little bird was so tiny, he could hardly believe such beautiful music was pouring from its beak.

As he watched, the bird fluttered from the sky, landing on his outstretched palms.

"If only you'd stay," Henry whispered, cupping his hands and cradling the tiny bird. "I'd love to have something to care for." But then he thought of his grim, lonely tower. No bird should be caged in such a place.

"Fly away, bird," he said. "Be free and happy." He opened his hands, let the lark go, and watched it rise far up into the sky.

The next morning, when he woke in his own room, the sunlight streaming in through the window, he heard a faint singing.

"It's the lark!" he realized. "It's come back."

After that, the lark hovered by the tower all the time, singing its song, and every time Henry heard it, he smiled, happy as a king.

Henry kept exploring and he kept reading. He read about the living world, and about history, and battles, and kings and queens, and it made him remember that he, too, was a prince.

"Shall I ever be a king?" he asked his nanny, one day.

"You should be a king," she replied solemnly. And she told him the story of his parents dying, and how his uncle had snatched the throne.

"Then he sent us away to the tower," she finished, sadly. "And there's nothing we can do about it. We'll both end our days here."

"How could my uncle do such a thing?" Henry thought, angrily. "I was a helpless baby. My nanny was powerless… But if I am a king, maybe there *is* something I could do."

He thought about this, long and hard. At last, he knew where he would start. "I'll travel on my magic cloak," he decided, "only I won't just look for beautiful things, but *everything*, good and bad, so I can understand the world better."

He flung out his cloak so that it settled on the stone floor. "Are you ready, Godmother?" he said.

"I am ready," came the reply, like a ripple of gentleness in the gloomy tower.

At Henry's command, the cloak flew over mountains, on and on, further than he had ever gone before, until he reached a great city. He heard a murmur, like a hive of bees, and soon he saw that the noise came from people and traffic and great factories, filled with clanking machines, belching out plumes of black smoke.

He saw dirty alleyways, and homeless men and women, and hungry children…

He saw dirty alleyways, and homeless men
and women, and hungry children… They were
bewildering, dreadful sights for a boy who had
never seen anything like it.

"I don't understand," he said.

"This is your city," whispered his Godmother's
voice on the breeze.

The magic cloak flew on and stopped at a huge,
stately building by an open window. Henry heard
someone say, "The King is dead."

Henry had always thought a king must be a very
splendid person, handsome, and strong. But here,
through the window, he saw a magnificent bed,
and on it, a small, still figure, not frightening, not
powerful, but lonely and silent. All Henry's anger
vanished and instead he felt pity for this small man,
whom he realized must have been his uncle.

"Did you enjoy what you stole?" Henry
wondered, as he gazed at him. "Did you do any
good wearing the crown?"

A great roar erupted from the streets.

"The King is dead!"

"Down with the King!"

"Revolution!"

At once, the streets began to fill with angry people, shouting over each other. Swiftly, the magic cloak turned around and flew away from the city, and back to the tower.

More than ever, Henry wanted to see his nanny – but the tower was empty. She had gone.

Henry looked outside and saw hoofprints on the sandy, stony earth, far below. He guessed that the soldier who brought their food had come, and taken his nanny away with him.

Now Henry was utterly alone. There was silence all around him.

"I can't stay here," he said aloud, "stuck in this tower. I want the chance to do something in the world…" And at the sound of his own voice, ringing around the tower, he knew the time had come to leave. He had no nanny to stay for. His uncle was dead. He would summon up his courage and return to the city. Then he would ask the people if they would have him as their King.

Henry laid out his magic cloak, but before he could give the command, he heard the sound of a trumpet, very bold and grand. Looking down, he saw a procession, with his nanny at the very head of it.

"Henry!" said his nanny, calling up to him, her voice rising through the still air. "The soldier came to tell me that your uncle had died, so I went to get help. I wanted the rightful King to sit on the throne. And you are that King!

Your uncle was a harsh, unkind ruler. The people remember you as a child and they want to welcome you back."

"I am ready," said Prince Henry. "I am ready to come back as your King."

Henry took one last look around the tower, saying goodbye to those four rooms, saying goodbye to his old life. "I wish I could say goodbye to my Godmother," he thought.

But then he heard a whisper in the shadows – his Godmother's voice. "Goodbye, King Henry," she said, her voice echoing around the tower.

"Goodbye," he replied. "And thank you."

"And now I am free," thought Henry. "Free to live my life at last."

And as the procession of horses and carriages brought the King back to the kingdom, Henry smiled to hear a lark, flying high above them, its soaring song filling the air.

Did Henry make a good King? Well, he tried. He learned how to take advice as well as give it and he always listened.

The wonderful craftspeople of his country made him a chair with wheels, so he could go everywhere. He was able to do good things, just as he had always wanted. As for the magic cloak… Now he was King, with a kingdom to rule, he had less time for flying. But every now and then, on moonlit nights, Henry would take out his cloak and chant the words he had learned all those years ago. *Abracadabra, dum di dum…* and away he flew.

Well, wouldn't you?

This story was first published in 1877. The author, Mary Molesworth, wrote it under the pen name, Ennis Graham.

The Cuckoo Clock

In an old town, in a cobbled street, shaded by ancient trees with twisting branches, there was a very old house. Such a house you'd never find nowadays, for it belonged to a time gone by. And the ladies who lived there were so old it seemed they could never get any older, and that they had outlived the possibility of change.

But one day, at last, there did come a change. One winter's evening, a little girl arrived. Her name was Rosie. She'd been living with her parents abroad, but her mother had died the year before, and her father had decided it was time for her to visit England, the country he still thought of as home.

"You'll love it there," he said. "And it's not forever. Soon I'll come and join you."

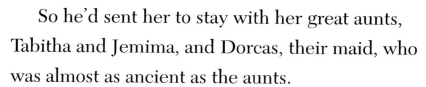

"When?" Rosie had asked.

"In six months, maybe…"

Six months? That seemed a lifetime away.

"Be brave," said her father. "I know you can."

So he'd sent her to stay with her great aunts, Tabitha and Jemima, and Dorcas, their maid, who was almost as ancient as the aunts.

When Rosie arrived, she gazed up at the old, old house, and felt a coldness settle inside of her, deep in the pit of her stomach. "What will my new life be like?" she wondered.

Her aunts greeted her kindly, and after supper Dorcas showed her upstairs into a little bedroom where a warm fire flickered welcomingly.

"It's all so strange," Rosie thought, as she tucked herself in for the night. "It's nothing like home. I don't feel I belong here at all."

Rosie was so tired, she fell asleep straight away. But she woke in the night to hear a *Cuckoo! Cuckoo!* ringing through the darkness. *Where did the sound come from? Did her aunts keep a cuckoo in a cage?* She couldn't work it out.

She asked them at breakfast.

"Not in a cage, my dear. In a clock," said Great Aunt Tabitha, beaming.

"She's so like Rosalie, her grandmother!" smiled Great Aunt Jemima. "You were named after her, you know."

"Don't say I'm like her," thought Rosie, squirming. "I'm not like anyone but *me*."

Rosie couldn't remember her grandmother, and she didn't like the thought of being compared to someone she had never really known.

"We'll show you the clock," said the aunts, and they led Rosie down twisting corridors, through a big room they called the saloon, hung with faded yellow silk – and into a little side room. Here, on one wall, was what looked like a miniature house made of carved wood, with a roof. It had a tiny door hidden above its clock face, and as Rosie watched, the cuckoo flew out and sang his cry, *Cuckoo...* nine times, flapping his wings as if he was saying hello.

"He never makes a mistake," said Great Aunt Tabitha. "All these years. He was made by your grandmother's grandfather, the old clockmaker."

"What's more," said Great Aunt Jemima, "your grandmother always said it was a *magic* clock, and would bring good luck to its owners. It's true. There's a friendly feeling in this house."

"There's an *old* feeling to this house," Rosie muttered under her breath.

"You'll get to know this room well, Rosie," said Great Aunt Tabitha. "You'll be doing your lessons here. We've engaged a tutor for you, Mr. Whitehead. And the cuckoo, always on time, always working, will set you a good example."

"Lessons!" thought Rosie, with a shudder. And the aunts talking about being stuck in a room, always working… Urgh!

Every day after that, Mr. Whitehead, a man as old as the aunts, taught Rosie in a voice that droned on and on. Rosie became grumpier and grumpier. There were no children anywhere for her to play with.

It was just her, and a houseful of old people, and her lessons. Finally she couldn't bear it any more…

One morning, at eleven o'clock, when she was all alone in the room, with another day of lessons stretching out before her, she heard the cuckoo again. It was as if he was crowing *work hard! work hard!* at her. And before she knew what she was doing, Rosie picked up the nearest, heaviest book and threw it at the little bird, shouting, "GO AWAY!"

The door snapped shut, mid-cuckoo. Rosie froze, appalled. *What had she done? Had she broken the clock?* She waited, tensely, until twelve o'clock, but though the clock ticked on, the cuckoo was silent. At lunch time, she sat with her aunts who were so upset, they forgot she was there.

"Seventy years… and never missed an hour,"

quavered Great Aunt Jemima.

"We're getting old, sister, perhaps it is to remind us of this," said Great Aunt Tabitha.

They wept together, and Dorcas came in to tell Rosie to play in the garden.

"I don't want to play outside," thought Rosie. "It's freezing cold. There's still frost on the grass. And I haven't anyone to play with. This house and the garden are just the same. *Dull. Cold. Miserable.*"

It was a strange afternoon. Rosie knew it was all her fault that the clock was broken – and her fault too that the aunts were so unhappy.

"Can't it be mended?" she asked Dorcas.

"No clockmaker these days would know how," Dorcas replied.

But that night, Rosie woke to hear a faint *Cuckoo!*

"He's alive!" she thought. "I must see him. I must!" And she jumped out of bed in her bare feet, running through the twisting passages, pushing away her fear of the flickering shadows.

"I'm sorry, Cuckoo," she said, when she finally

reached the clock. "I was just so angry. I didn't mean to hurt you…"

The door opened. Out flew the cuckoo.

"You didn't hurt *me*," he said, in a sing-song voice. "You hurt my feelings. However, we'll say no more about it, since you're sorry. Why were you angry?"

A *magic* cuckoo, Rosie realized, just as her grandmother had said. At once, she felt a funny, fluttery feeling in her tummy. "But the only sensible thing to do," she decided, "is to answer the cuckoo's question."

"I was angry because there's no one to play with," Rosie explained. "Even when I go into the garden, there's nothing to do."

"I'll see what can be done," replied the cuckoo. "Now, back to bed." He gave her a nod, and chirped *Cuckoo!*

At breakfast, the aunts were wreathed in smiles as they sat listening to the cuckoo chiming the hour.

"I'm glad the cuckoo's come back," said Rosie.

"He'll never go away again."

"You are so like your grandmother, Rosalie," said Great Aunt Tabitha. "She watched your great great grandfather make that clock, you know."

"And she always treasured it," added Great Aunt Jemima.

"Why are you always saying I'm like my grandmother? I'm not old and wrinkly!"

"She was younger than you when she came here," said Great Aunt Jemima, gently. "Everyone loved her, she was so kind."

In reply, Rosie just shrugged. She was nothing like her grandmother. She was nothing like her stuffy old aunts. The only good thing about being here was the cuckoo.

All day, Rosie wondered what the cuckoo was planning for her. Sure enough, that night, she was woken again by his greeting, *Cuckoo! Cuckoo!*

She ran to the clock, down the chilly moonlit passages, bathed in shadow.

"Good, you're here," said the cuckoo, peeping out of his door. "Climb up the clock chains and come inside, and we'll talk."

"Climb up!" exclaimed Rosie. "But I'm huge and the clock is tiny!"

"Nonsense," said the cuckoo. "Big and small, it's all just a way of thinking. Try."

Rosie swung herself up, how, she didn't know, and found herself in a snug little room all covered in red velvet, soft as moss, with comfortable chairs.

"So you want to play?" said the cuckoo.

"Yes," said Rosie eagerly. "And to be somewhere different, where it's not dark, like my aunts' house; not winter, not old, like everything is here."

"Very well," said the cuckoo. And he opened another little door that seemed to lead into the wall. "Come this way, and you shall see…"

…What did she see? The loveliest, most sunshiny garden ever. It was almost like being home again, only even more magical. Emerald grass, a little stream, and flowers everywhere. And fluttering among the flowers, thousands of butterflies. The garden was alive with them.

"Welcome to Butterfly Land," said the cuckoo.

"Look at them all," exclaimed Rosie, her voice full of wonder. "They're dancing on the flowers."

As she spoke, the butterflies came away from the flowers, swooping towards her. She could see the patterns on their wings, orange, purple, blue, all shining, iridescent, in the sunlight.

"Oh, Rosie!" said the cuckoo. "The butterflies are inviting you to their ball."

"But I can't go in my nightdress!" said Rosie.

"The butterflies will help," replied the cuckoo. The butterflies came closer, landing, feather-light, on her head, her arms… and then she realized. They were dressing her… with themselves! They settled in a belt of blue and yellow around her waist and fell in waves about her. Prettiest of all was the wreath in her hair, and her shoes, which they made by perching softly on her bare feet.

And then, best of all, Rosie found she could fly. Whether it was the hundreds of butterflies she was wearing, flapping their wings for her, or whether it was the cuckoo's magic, she didn't know, but she was part of the dance, swirling through the blue air.

Then they all, butterflies, cuckoo, and Rosie, settled down at a long table where nectar was laid out. Rosie ate hers with a dainty spoon. She thought she'd never forget its creamy sweetness.

"Clap, to show you like it," said the cuckoo, and as Rosie clapped, once, twice, the butterflies rose into a vast feathery cloud. On her third clap, they – and the garden – disappeared altogether. Rosie looked around, and found she was in her own bed, with dawn just breaking at the start of a new day.

Rosie smiled at her aunts over breakfast. She even tried to pay attention to Mr. Whitehead in her lessons. She had a small bud of happiness inside her, melting the coldness. It was there every time she thought of the cuckoo. "Perhaps this house isn't *so* bad after all," she told herself.

After lunch, the sun came out from behind the clouds and Rosie longed to go outside. But as she was putting on her shoes, her aunts heard her sneezing.

"You can't go out if you have a cold, Rosie," they told her. "You had best stay inside this afternoon."

"I'm fine," said Rosie, but at that unfortunate moment, she gave a little cough.

"No, you're not," said Great Aunt Tabitha. And after that, no matter how much Rosie told them it was nothing, they insisted on tucking her up in an armchair by the fire in the snug side room, and gave her cakes, and delicious hot blackcurrant drinks and their special tansy tea. She knew it was kind of them, but she still felt cramped and cross, and couldn't bring herself to say, "Thank you."

"Of course I could have gone outside," she muttered to herself. "It probably won't be sunny again for weeks. I've hardly got a cold at all."

And then, even though she was on her own, she let out a loud, "HUMPH!"

At once, the clock door flew open and out came the cuckoo. "Hello, Rosie," he sang. "What would you like to do today?"

"I don't know," said Rosie. "I can't go anywhere. I'm stuck in this horrible chair."

"I could show you pictures, if you like," said the cuckoo, "of this house when your great great grandfather made the clock."

"I suppose that would be better than nothing," Rosie said grudgingly.

"Very well," said the cuckoo, ignoring her grumpiness. "Close your eyes. I'm going to sing."

Rosie obeyed. The cuckoo's song was beautiful, soft and dreamy, making her think of rippling brooks, and insects buzzing, and everything humming, and she fell asleep.

When she woke, the room had disappeared in a misty cloud, all except herself in her armchair. She was in a workroom, hung with strange, wonderful clocks. One was carved like the sun, another like the moon, while another had a fiddler playing his violin as the hour struck. A man, very old, wearing an apron, was sitting at a table looking at something with a magnifying glass, surrounded by tiny nails and dials and hammers.

In ran a little girl, with long hair down her back, and jingling with bracelets and necklaces.

"Well, my darling?" he asked.

"You're working very hard, Grandfather."

"All for you, Rosalie. These clocks shall be yours to sell, when I am dead. But the cuckoo clock you must never sell. It will last long after you and I are gone, and one day, perhaps it will remind your

"You're working very hard, Grandfather."

grandchildren of the old clockmaker."

"No one could ever forget you, Grandfather!" The little girl flung herself into his arms, and the picture faded.

Another picture. This time it was a party. Rosie recognized the room: it was the big saloon, but oh! how different it looked. It was bright with candlelight, and the yellow silk curtains looked fresh and new. Bouquets of flowers filled the air with their scent. There were ladies and gentlemen laughing and dancing to merry music.

The Cuckoo Clock

"And those are your aunts," said the cuckoo, nodding at two ladies, young and handsome.

"I imagined them as always old!" gasped Rosie. But she didn't notice them for long. She was staring at a young woman in a red dress, who seemed brimming over with happiness. Her very steps had joy in them. She was dancing with a young man, who gazed at her lovingly.

"Do you know who that is, Rosie?" asked the cuckoo, a gleam in his eyes.

Rosie shook her head.

"That's Rosalie, your grandmother."

She looked at the young woman again, and saw that they had the same eyes, the same smile.

But then the picture began to fade. She was alone in her armchair, in the little side room with the fire flickering in the hearth. And just at that moment, her aunts came in.

Rosie's questions tumbled out in a rush. "Where did my grandmother meet my grandfather? Was it here, in the saloon, at the party? And my grandmother was so sweet when she was a little girl, when she lived with her grandfather…"

"How do you know these old stories?" asked Great Aunt Tabitha.

"The cuckoo showed me," said Rosie, and when Great Aunt Jemima murmured, "The child *is* like Rosalie," Rosie didn't mind at all.

"Thank you for my tea, and for the cake," said Rosie. "I feel much better."

Her aunts beamed at her. "Our tansy tea," they said proudly, "just the thing for a cold."

Seeing their smiles, their faces lit up with remembering, Rosie felt another little glow of happiness inside.

Soon, the weather began to change. Winter faded and springtime rolled in, full of wildflowers and fresh green shoots. Rosie had never seen an English spring before, and she ran around the garden and the fields beyond, discovering bluebells and violets, rabbits and squirrels.

"It's another sort of magic," she thought. "Not the cuckoo's magic, but watching things grow, and smelling the flowers, and listening to birdsong – it is a little magical."

She gathered flowers for her aunts, to make them smile, and they loved seeing her rosy cheeks and cheerful face. She was much happier, but… "I still haven't anyone to play with," she thought.

She hadn't seen the cuckoo for weeks, but one warm day, outside in the garden, she heard, clear as a bell, the familiar *Cuckoo! Cuckoo!*

"Where are you, Cuckoo?" she cried.

There was no answer.

A rustling in the bushes made her turn around, expecting to see him. But it was a boy, younger than her, creeping through the undergrowth, his clothes torn by the brambles.

"Did *you* hear the cuckoo?" he asked. "I want to find him!"

Rosie was astonished. It was so long since she'd spoken to a child. His name was Billy, he told her, and he'd come to live at the farm nearby with his mother, who'd been very ill.

"What do you know about the cuckoo?" she asked him.

"He's called to me, lots of times. I think he called me today to come and play with you. I don't know anyone around here."

"I don't know anyone either," said Rosie. And, even though Billy was younger than she was, as they began talking and running about the fields together, Rosie felt as if she were coming alive again.

"This is going to sound strange," she told Billy. "But I feel as if I've been asleep all winter – in a strange kind of dream."

"I felt like that when my mother was ill," said Billy. "As if time was standing still, and I was just waiting for her to get better."

"Is she better now?" asked Rosie, hoping so much, for Billy, that she was.

Billy nodded. "She's even started noticing things again – like how I still can't read properly. I wish I could learn and surprise her."

"I'll teach you!" said Rosie. "Let's meet by this hedge tomorrow, and we'll begin."

When Rosie arrived home, she told her aunts about meeting Billy.

"A boy!" cried Great Aunt Tabitha.

"One we don't know!" gasped Great Aunt Jemima. "We haven't even met his mother."

"What does that matter?" demanded Rosie.

"Of course it matters," said Great Aunt Tabitha.

"Well I'm seeing him tomorrow," declared Rosie, stamping her foot. "You *can't* tell me not to."

"You're being very rude, Rosie," said Great Aunt Jemima. "You certainly won't be allowed to meet him tomorrow."

Rosie ran to her room, slammed the door and flung herself on her bed, crying. "Poor Billy," she was thinking. "He'll go to the hedge, and he won't know why I'm not there."

It was stormy, that night, with raindrops hammering on the window panes. Rosie went to the window, watching the wild clouds racing. In the darkness, she could just make out a bird, huddled on the ledge. She opened the latch and in flew the cuckoo. "It's you!" she said. "What were you doing out in the cold?"

"Seeing if you still wanted me," said the cuckoo.

"I'll *always* want you, Cuckoo," said Rosie.

"We'll see about that," the cuckoo replied, flying around the room. "Now, don't worry about your aunts. I'll work my magic on them so you can see Billy again." Then he stopped flying and perched on the windowsill. "How about another adventure?"

Rosie nodded eagerly. "Where to?" she asked.

"To the other side of the moon," announced the cuckoo. "Climb on my back."

Off they flew. Small as he was, the moment Rosie touched him, she could lie comfortably on his feathers, and they soared upwards. Nearer and nearer the stars they came.

There was such a rushing sound in her ears that Rosie shut her eyes, and when she opened

them, she was by a strange, silent sea. But there were no waves, and an odd, muted light.

"Is it moonlight?" Rosie asked.

"Not exactly," said the cuckoo.

"Is there any life here?"

The air was so still, as though nothing had disturbed it since time began.

"There may have been once, and may be again," came the cuckoo's reply.

"It's a long way from home," said Rosie. "I feel I've been away for fifty years. Have I, Cuckoo?"

"Your ideas of time being long or short, big and little, far and near, are all a matter of fancy."

"I don't think I understand," said Rosie. The cuckoo seemed to be saying time didn't matter at all, but he came from a clock. It was his job to measure out the hours.

"Past and present, even the future," said the cuckoo, "they all come together."

That made Rosie think of her grandmother. She'd never known her, but now she felt she had, at least a little. And being in this strange, other-wordly place, she began to feel as if she really belonged in that old house, just as much as the cuckoo in his clock.

"Thank you for bringing me here," she said to the cuckoo. "You are the kindest of friends. But I think I'm ready to go home now."

"Then home we'll go," said the cuckoo. "I know a shortcut."

A boat was floating towards them, with a pair of oars inside. The cuckoo grasped the oars with his tiny feet. *Splish! Splash! Splish! Splash!*

As Rosie counted the soft dipping of the oars, she fell asleep…

…and woke in her own bed.

Her first thought was how rude she'd been to
Great Aunt Tabitha and Great Aunt Jemima. "I had
better say sorry," she decided.

But they were sorry too. And they had a surprise
for her: Billy and his mother were
coming to the house for tea.

When they arrived, Billy
smiled at her and she smiled
back. She knew she'd found
a true friend.

The Cuckoo Clock

That night Rosie dreamed the cuckoo came to her one last time.

"You don't need me now. You've started to belong. And that's better than the butterflies, better even than your faithful old cuckoo."

Rosie tried to thank him, but he flew away.

Cuckoo! Cuckoo! he sang, and somehow the last cuckoo sounded like goodbye. Her eyes filled with tears. She'd see him again every time he sang the hours, but the magic had gone. She knew she was going to be happy, very happy, in what felt like home now, with her new friend, but she was crying for the one she'd said farewell to, even though he was only a cuckoo in a clock.

First published as A Little Girl in a Book, *the author wrote the story 'For Penelope... to keep the sunbeams always in her heart.'*

The Girl in the Book

Once, there was a girl named Emily who loved to read. She read everything she could: family stories, magic stories, animal stories, but best of all were adventure stories. She liked to think of herself as all the heroes who had amazing experiences in faraway lands.

Emily longed to travel to blazing hot deserts, ice-cold realms and vast empty wildernesses. She wished she could tame bears and hyenas, ride on elephants and run with tigers. She wanted to know what it felt like to escape a hurricane, a forest fire, a flood, an exploding volcano!

The heroes in her books were always wonderfully brave and full of cleverness. They rescued their friends, foraged food and cooked over fires they made by rubbing flints over straw. They built shelters and they never, ever complained.

"They're not like me," thought Emily. "Lucky things. I wish I could be like them…"

Emily's life could not have been more different. She lived in a small house in a quiet street full of other identical houses. She had one sister, Isabella, who was grown up and wrote books. Isabella sat in her room all day, scribbling away, and never played with her at all.

Emily's father and mother were quiet, busy people who liked being alone with their thoughts.

Her father was an artist, and her mother was a professor. Her father sat painting in a studio, and her mother sat in a study, teaching and learning. They were all happy and occupied, and expected Emily to be the same. They didn't want her to bring friends back to the house, as it would be "too disruptive" they said, and create too much noise.

So Emily went to school, and came home, and read her books, and that was how she spent her days. And she couldn't help worrying that she wasn't nearly as interesting as the children in her books. She wasn't especially witty. She wasn't an amazing athlete. She'd never run along a narrow branch to cross a raging waterfall, or plunged in and out of deadly whirlpools, or raced away from a pack of hungry lions. She was just an ordinary girl in an ordinary house in an ordinary town.

But in her imagination she went everywhere. She sprinted, swam, jumped, rescued wild beasts, and dodged danger over and over again. But sometimes, just sometimes, she felt that even this wasn't enough.

"If I lived in a book," she thought, "I'd be brave and clever and interesting. I'd always say the right thing, and act in a wonderful way at just the right moment. Everyone would look up to me. Perhaps I'd discover things about myself I never even knew…"

One day, when Emily had read so much that even she was tired of reading, she went up to her sister's bedroom, longing for some human company. But Isabella ignored her. She just stayed at her desk, writing. She didn't even look up.

"Hello," said Emily, drumming her fingers on the windowsill.

"I'm busy," said Isabella. "Sorry."

"Don't you get bored, just writing and writing?"

Isabella shook her head, and went on writing.

"Well, I'm bored," said Emily. She wasn't sure that Isabella had really heard her, so she went on talking, as if she were thinking aloud. "If I could be in a book, an adventure book, I'd be different. I could do anything. My life would be exciting, and I'd be a hero."

"Hmm," said Isabella, looking up for the first time, and giving Emily a very odd smile. "Really?"

"You're a hopeless sister," said Emily crossly, and she went out, slamming the door behind her.

What Emily didn't see was the way Isabella kept smiling after she'd left the room, or the light in her eyes when she started to write again…

Just a few weeks later, Emily began to feel strange. A sort of stiffness spread over her limbs, and sometimes she found herself saying things that weren't like her, or didn't seem to fit with her life, as if she were rehearsing lines in a play.

One morning, at breakfast, she heard herself say, "I can climb to the top of that palm tree." Then, at school in the playground, she said, "I'm

a strong swimmer. I can swim to that far-out reef."
And, of course, there hadn't been a palm tree or a
reef anywhere in sight. She wasn't even a particularly
strong swimmer. Emily began to wonder if it was
because she was on her own too much, or if she had
simply read too many stories. This went on for some
days, but no one else seemed to notice.

Then, one day, without any warning, Emily
woke up to find that everything around her had
changed. When she opened her eyes, she wasn't in
her bedroom at all, but on the deck of a ship. White
sails billowed in the wind above her, clouds scudded
across an azure blue sky, while waves splashed and
foamed around the sides of the ship.

It was a very grand ship, Emily soon realized, full
of people in beautiful clothes and sparkling jewels.
And when she looked down at herself, she saw
that she, too, was in a very grand dress, laced with
diamonds. There was a band playing and servants
handing out delicious little cakes on silver platters.

"Gosh," thought Emily.

But before she could really take it all in, a raggedy ship sailed into view, its black flags flaunting a skull and crossbones.

"Pirates!" cried everyone on the ship.

"All hands on deck!" shouted the Captain, and they sailed as fast as they could in the opposite direction.

But the pirate ship was gaining on them, and very soon six pirates, in striped jerseys, black trousers and bare feet, leaped on board the ship, grabbed Emily and ran off with her to their ship.

They were laughing evil laughter and crowing with delight at all the jewels they'd stolen. Then they bundled Emily below deck and all she could hear were stomping feet and sea shanties, as the pirates celebrated. There was a baby, too, whom the pirates had kidnapped along with Emily. The baby lay next to Emily, gurgling.

At first, Emily felt terribly afraid. What would happen to her? What *had* happened to her? Then the remarkable reason suddenly flashed over her: Isabella had put her into a book. She remembered her sister's odd smile. She was in Isabella's adventure story, she was sure of it.

"I'm going to enjoy myself," she decided – except she found she couldn't say the words out loud. Maybe those weren't the words in the book…

Maybe she could only say the words that had been written for her! But Emily soon decided that didn't matter, because the book was full of adventures. There wasn't a moment to feel bored.

The pirates had captured her and the baby to ransom them, so they'd get a lot of money. But even though they were out and out villains, and extremely wicked, Emily found she could deal with them easily. In fact, they admired her courage so much that they begged her to stay with them forever, catching fish and making them laugh and be merry. They even promised, under her guidance, to be less wicked in the future.

The girl-in-the-book Emily thought seriously about their offer. She liked living out at sea, with the wind blowing through her hair, and the sun on her face. But, in the end, Emily-in-the-book decided she didn't want to spend her entire life with pirates. It was time to leave.

The pirates, however, began to insist that she stayed, and things were getting awkward, when along came a terrible storm. Their boat was nearly overturned and they were all thrown into the sea. Emily nearly drowned. The water filled her mouth and nostrils, making her choke, but she managed to splutter and cough the water from her lungs, and she recovered quickly.

One of the pirates was a weak swimmer and he nearly drowned too. But Emily-the-hero saved him and hauled him back on board, forgiving him, and all of them, for capturing her. Then, when they were all still recovering from the storm, she cut loose one of the little rowing boats hanging from the side of the ship, and, taking the baby, she made her escape from the pirates.

In the little boat, Emily plunged through tempestuous waves, mountains high. She rowed past sharks and whales, and through pods of dolphins who frolicked enchantingly by her side. Far off she could see a shoreline.

By now she was parched with thirst and the relentless sun beat painfully on her head.

*In the little boat, Emily plunged through
tempestuous waves, mountains high.*

Her limbs ached, and her eyes were painfully sore from all the salt water. She was also very tired. But she kept going, chatting to the baby to keep him happy (although he didn't have much to say back), until, after many hours of rowing, she and the baby finally reached the shore.

Emily crawled over rocks covered in sharp, spiky shells and slippery seaweed, keeping tight hold of the baby, and, at last, they were safe on dry land once more. Her determination and stamina had carried them through. She'd done it! Emily-the-hero was a winner! It was a glorious feeling and Emily revelled in it.

But there was still work to be done. Emily was now on a deserted island. Quickly, she found fresh water in a stream, and a tree plentiful with delicious ripe fruit. She drank and ate, helping the baby, who remained cheerful and gurgled happily.

The island turned out to be full of wolves, who growled menacingly as they crept out of the undergrowth at dusk. They sniffed her, creeping

closer, baring their fangs.

But Emily-the-hero's intuitive gentleness and understanding of their ways made them accept her. The growls turned into a murmur of welcome. Soon she and the baby were treated as part of the pack.

The wolves brought her meat, which she cooked over a fire, made by rubbing two flints together. She was good at this. At night, she slept among the wolves, their bodies protecting her, their eyes shining yellow in the darkness, just like the stars that glimmered in the clear night sky above.

When Emily first reached this point in the

adventure story, she thought as she settled down with the wolves and the baby, "I do hope the book has a happy ending. I'm sure it will. Books like this always do."

It did.

After two weeks on the island, a ship sailed towards the bay. Emily quickly lit a fire, and its smoke signal drew the ship ashore. She was taken aboard, and hailed as a hero. She learned there had been a worldwide search for her, and the baby, and she was restored to her loving family, famous throughout the world for her unfaltering courage and incredible abilities.

The book's final paragraph was about Emily and everyone in the book living Happily Ever After.

And although Emily could only say the words written for her in the book, she could still think her own thoughts. "I've been brave!" she told herself. "It's all been easy! I've known what to do, and I've done it. I've endured hardship and danger, and I've rescued the baby, and I've triumphed! I am a little exhausted, though, after all that."

Then the person who had been reading the book finished it and shut it up with a snap. Emily was thankful to close her eyes and go to sleep. The pirates, the wolves, the baby, the sea and the storm were all mercifully silenced.

But very soon, someone else picked up the book and began reading. Emily was jerked awake, and found herself back at the beginning of the story, starting with the charming ship and its parties. On came the pirates, laughing and singing, grabbing her and bundling her onto their boat. It wasn't nearly as exciting the second time around, because she knew what was going to happen.

She didn't really want to get soaking wet all over again, being tossed into the sea when the storm came, but of course she had no choice. And her boat ride with the dolphins, holding the baby, had lost its thrill. She just wanted to get to the island, out of that hot sun, and stop rowing.

She still liked being with the wolves, though,

and enjoyed bringing the rescue ship ashore with her smoke signals, and being reunited with her family, and everyone saying how wonderful she was.

Still, she was glad that this reader read the book very quickly, so that she could get some rest when they'd finished it.

She didn't rest for long. Immediately she'd come to the end of her adventures, the book was handed to another reader. And then it all started again.

And again.

And again.

The book was proving to be a very popular one. Emily was glad, for Isabella's sake, that Isabella had written a best-seller, but every time someone read it, Emily went through all her adventures again. And she got very tired of it.

"Do I have to spend the rest of my life with pirates and shipwrecks?" she wondered. "It never stops. And though I like babies, and this one *is* sweet, I don't want to look after it *all* the time."

After a few hundred people had read the book, Emily had really had enough. She knew the entire book by heart. Every word. And the worst part was never being able to say what she wanted. She wanted to talk to the pirates more, to ask them why they'd become pirates, and where they'd come from, and about their families. And she wanted to learn more about fishing. And again, she was getting really interested in living with the wolves, and wished she could have spent longer with them.

There was so much to learn and discover – she wanted to know about the birds that flew over the island, and the flowers she'd never seen grow anywhere else, but she had to obey the storyline. Isabella hadn't written anything about all the things that now entranced Emily. The book was just an adventure story, pure and simple, with no proper thoughts or feelings explored.

"It's not enough," thought Emily. "I hate not being able to say what I want. I don't want words put in my mouth. I need to speak for myself."

Gradually, an idea dawned on her. She must escape from the book. She had a feeling it was going to take far more bravery and courage than her character in the adventure story. All brave-Emily-the-hero had to do was to follow the story. But to get out of the story, she was going to have to take a leap into the unknown. Where would she be leaping to? Another book? Or a leap to nowhere? Would she vanish altogether? Or might she get home? There was no way of telling.

More importantly, how was she going to escape? Every line in the book was set in stone. There was no way she could actually change the plot. Somehow, she'd have to strike out for herself! She decided to begin by jumping into the sea from the pirate ship before the storm. Then she could somehow swim away. But it didn't turn out like that…

The person reading the book flipped over the pages extremely fast at this point, as though the chapter was so gripping that it had to be gobbled up. Before she could do anything, Emily found herself flung out of the ship as usual, soaked through, into the massive, seething waves. This was the worst part in the book. She'd always hated the water filling her mouth and nose, and not being able to breathe.

Then the person reading the book handed it to someone else, saying, "There! Read that exact part, where I've been reading, about the shipwreck and the storm and nearly drowning."

This was too much for Emily. Nearly drowning all over again, WITH NO REST IN BETWEEN! She wasn't going to allow it. She was filled, suddenly, with waves, not of seawater in her nose, but of DETERMINATION. Nothing was going to stop her now. As the waves rocked the boat, Emily clung on tight to the rigging, refusing to be thrown into the water. The pirates stared at her in surprise.

"It's no good looking at me like that," she said.

"I'm tired of this. I'm not going to keep saying the words in the book. I'm going to say my own words, beginning now."

The pirates didn't know what to do. They started shouting, as though Emily had unleashed them from their book-spell, and they could use their own words too. "Behave! Get back in the water and carry on with nearly drowning! You're ruining the book!"

"I'm going to leave the book," said Emily. "Why don't you come too?"

But the pirates looked terrified. "It's safer here," they mumbled. "We know what's going to happen."

"Who cares for safety?" cried Emily. "This book's too predictable. Dull. I need something more."

All the pirates, and the sharks and the dolphins and the wolves, and even the baby came together and flung themselves on Emily as if to drag her back to where she should be in the book. Meanwhile, the sea swirled menacingly, getting on with its ferocious storm. The roar of the water and howls from the animals and yells from the pirates rose to a crescendo.

"There's something very odd about this book," she heard someone say, like a sound from far away. "It seems all mixed-up. And strangely noisy."

Emily knew this was her moment. The book-spell had completely broken. She had a chance to get out and she had to take it.

"GOODBYE!" she shouted to the pirates and the wolves and the dolphins and the sharks and the baby. Summoning all her strength, she leaped up and out of the boat…

It was like flying. She didn't land in the sea as she'd half-feared. Instead, she leaped out of the page, out of the book, and found herself…

…in Isabella's bedroom. As usual, Isabella was writing busily. Emily stood breathless before her.

"You put me in your book."

"I did," said Isabella. "Didn't you like it?"

"Well," said Emily, "I loved it at first. It was exciting. But after the third or fourth time, it was dull! I had to do the same things, and I couldn't speak for myself."

"Oh," said Isabella, thinking it over. "Yes, I can see how the excitement might not last."

"But thank you for putting me in your book," said Emily, not wanting to sound ungrateful. "It was kind of you. Sisterly."

"I wanted to make you happy," said Isabella. "But what are you going to do now? If you were bored by your life before, then you will be again. Nothing has really changed."

"Oh but it has," said Emily, smiling. "Now I know I'm not boring or ordinary. And what's more, I'm even braver than the heroes in my books, because I can think for myself."

"Bravo!" said Isabella, cheering.

"And now," said Emily, "I'm going to talk to Mother and Father about allowing me to have some friends over…" She paused a moment.

"Anything else?" asked Isabella.

"Yes," said Emily. "I think I'll try writing a book of my own…"

This story, by George MacDonald,
was first published in 1872.

The Princess and the Goblins

Princess Esme lived high in the mountains in a towering castle. Her mother had died when she was a baby, and although her father, the King, loved his daughter very much, he was often away, touring the kingdom, or in the city, attending to affairs of state.

Instead, Esme had her nanny, Lootie, to care for her, and the palace servants for company. She loved her mountain home, with its sparkling streams and cool, clear air, and the flowers that bloomed in spring, but one thing made her sad… She was never allowed outside after sunset. The ceiling in her bedroom was painted dark blue with silver stars, but she longed to be out in the night air, and lie on the ground beneath a canopy of real stars.

"I wish I could go out," she said one beautiful evening, watching the deepening shadows of the sunbeams fall on the mountains.

"You can't," said Lootie, her nanny. "You know the King forbids it."

"But *why* can't I go out?" pleaded Esme.

"You're too young to know why," said Lootie. "Now be a good girl, while I go about my chores."

But on this particular evening, Esme couldn't settle. She longed to explore, and if she couldn't go outside, she decided she would wander the castle. It was so huge, she knew there were turrets she had never visited before. So she slipped out of her room and through one door, and then another…

On and on she went, down endless passageways, up and down twisting stairs. Wherever she looked there were cobwebs draped like dusty necklaces, while the wind whistled around the turrets.

"I'm lost," she whispered after a while, stopping by yet another door and realizing, with rising panic, that she had no idea how to get back.

"I'm not afraid," she tried to tell herself. "I'm a princess and princesses are brave. I'll have to help myself."

Then, in the silence, came a whirring, humming noise. At first, Esme thought it was the wind, but as she followed the sound, it grew louder.

She climbed some stairs and the humming grew louder still. Esme opened the door where the sound seemed loudest…

Inside was a little room, with a lady, spinning. She had silver hair that hung in long waves to the floor, and a lamp above her, round as a ball and shining, as if with the brightest moonlight. There was a fire, too, which flickered with flames shaped like roses, piled up in a glowing red heap in the hearth.

"Come in, Esme," said the old lady.

"How do you know my name?"

"It's my name too," smiled the old lady. "I gave it to you when you were born. I am your great great grandmother."

"Have you always lived here, Great Great Grandmother?" asked Esme, her eyes wide.

"You can just call me *Grandmother*," the old lady replied, with a smile. "Yes, I've always lived here. I stay here so I can take care of you."

"But why have I never met you before?"

"Well, my dear," her grandmother replied, "you've never needed me before. Now, see what I've been spinning for you."

As she spoke, the grandmother held out a shimmering ball of white spun silk.

"Thank you," said Esme politely. "Is it for me to play with?"

"It's not a toy," said her grandmother, going to a cupboard. She took out a ring with a glittering stone that changed in the firelight from red to blue to green to white.

"It's beautiful," said Esme.

"It's a fire opal," said her grandmother. "Put it on your finger. It's yours."

"How lovely," exclaimed Esme, admiring it.

Her grandmother took the silk-spun ball and wound some silk around the ring. "There, Esme," she said. "Now you have it."

"No, Grandmother," Esme corrected her. "I have your ring, but *you* have my ball."

"You have the ball too," her grandmother replied, "fastened to the fire opal on the ring."

"I don't understand," said Esme.

"Feel its thread with your fingers."

Esme stretched out her hands into the air in front of her. With a cry of delight, she touched the strand. It glimmered briefly, then disappeared, but she could feel it between her fingers, as light and strong as spider silk.

"I can feel it!" she cried.

"When the ring glitters, follow the thread," said her grandmother. "It may take you to strange places, but you must trust it. While you hold it, I hold it too."

"I promise, Grandmother," said Esme. "It must be magic. Are you magic as well?"

"I'm old," her grandmother laughed.

"I thought being old meant being slow, and not able to see well. You're not like that."

"Being old means – or ought to mean – strength and wisdom, courage and beauty. I'm older than you can imagine. And I'm happy here, up in the rafters, with the cooing doves for company."

"Can I bring my nanny, Lootie, to see you?" asked Esme. "And my father, the King, when he next comes?"

"You can try," said her grandmother, "but I'm afraid they wouldn't believe you if you told them about me, or even be able to see me."

"But they *must* believe me," said Esme.

"We all want to be believed, and to be understood," said her grandmother. "But there is one thing that's much more important."

"What's that?" asked Esme.

"To understand other people. That's the beginning of kindness. Now shut your eyes, Esme. When you open them, you'll find yourself tucked up in your own bed."

Esme woke to find herself exactly where her grandmother had said, with moonlight shining through the curtains. A moment later, Lootie came bursting into her room.

"Oh you naughty girl," she exclaimed, half crying, half angry. "Why did you run off like that! Thank goodness you're safe. I was afraid–"

She broke off, abruptly.

"What were you afraid of?" asked Esme.

"Never mind that now," Lootie replied. "Where were you?"

"I went to see my great great grandmother who lives at the very top of the castle."

"Now don't go making up stories," said Lootie, wagging her finger.

"I'm not!" protested Esme. "Look at my ring. My great great grandmother gave it to me. And it has an invisible thread, too."

"You've probably always had that ring. And as for invisible thread… What nonsense!"

Esme began to feel cross, but then she remembered her grandmother's words. Perhaps it was too hard for Lootie to believe in magical great great grandmothers and invisible threads.

"Never mind," said Esme, "let's not argue. Shall we go for a walk tomorrow, up the mountain?"

"Let's!" said Lootie, hugging her close.

And so the next afternoon, they set off up the mountain. Esme jumped in the sparkling streams that tumbled and splashed down the slopes, and played with the wild goats and their kids. Neither she nor Lootie noticed the setting sun casting its long dark shadows.

"Look, Lootie!" cried Esme. "There's a strange little face looking at us."

Lootie took one look and turned pale with fright. "We mustn't be out a moment longer," she cried. She grabbed Esme by the hand and began to run.

"But what was it?" asked Esme. "And why are we running?"

Lootie didn't answer. She just ran faster than ever, until Esme tripped over a rock, grazing her hands and knees.

"Oh!" she cried, in a heap on the ground. "I'm bleeding and my clothes are torn. And I'm sure I can hear someone laughing. Who is it?" she called into the shadows.

"No one," said Lootie, trying to lift Esme to her feet. "Only the wind."

"Ha! Ha! *Lies*!" whispered a chorus of voices, echoing from the stones around the path.

"I'm sure I can hear something," said Esme, "and it *isn't* the wind."

By now, Lootie was shaking. "We're lost, and I don't know where we are and it's getting dark…"

Then, strolling towards them, came one of the boys who worked in the mountain mines. He was smudged and dirty, and he whistled as he walked.

"What are you doing out after dark?" said the boy. "You could get caught by the—"

"Shhh… Don't say the word!" hissed Lootie.

"Now, boy," she went on hurriedly, "do you know the way back to the castle?"

"Of course I do," said the boy.

"Then take us there. At once," ordered Lootie. "And Princess, don't listen to anything he says."

"I hope they didn't hear you call her *Princess*," whispered the boy. "If they did, they're sure to know her again. They're very clever. But I'll get you back. I know this path, and the castle isn't far."

The boy began to walk, with Lootie following him, Esme's hand clutched tightly in her own.

And that was when Esme saw them properly – strange, shadowy creatures, scattering before them across the path.

"I really can see something," she said. "What are they? Please tell me. I'd rather know than not…"

"Goblins, of course," said the boy, and he ran into their midst, stamping on their bare feet. At each stamp, there was a yell of rage, and the goblins dashed away into the shadows again.

Esme watched him in amazement.

"Goblins have hard heads," explained the boy, smiling at her as he spoke, "but very soft feet, and they hate having them stamped on! The other trick is not to be afraid."

"Where do they come from?" asked Esme, trying *very* hard not to be afraid.

"Goblins live deep in the mountains," replied the boy. "They like cold, dark places, and only come out at night. They hate people. They hate the miners who work in the mountains, but more than anything, they hate the King. We don't know the reason why, and I expect if you asked them, they wouldn't know either."

"But why did no one tell me about them?"

"We didn't want to worry you," said Lootie.

Before Esme could ask any more questions,

they reached the castle door. "Don't be out late again, Princess," warned the boy. "Goblins can be dangerous, you know."

Lootie hurried them inside but Esme turned back. "Wait!" she insisted. "We haven't thanked the boy yet. What's your name?" she asked him.

"Curdie."

"Thank you, Curdie," said Esme, hugging him.

"Really, Princess!" said Lootie. She hustled Esme inside and closed the door behind them.

Curdie left the castle and walked on, down the path to his little cottage. It was tiny and shabby, but his mother had made it a snug little heaven on the mountainside.

As he came in, his parents were at the table, with supper all laid out.

"The goblins have seen the Princess," Curdie told them, as he sat down to eat. "I'm worried about her. The castle people don't look after her properly."

"She should be protected," said his father. "We all know how much the goblins hate the King."

"Don't worry, Father," said Curdie. "I'm going to spend the night down the mine. That way I can listen in on the goblins' plans." He was thinking, too, that he could work while he was down there and earn extra money to buy his mother a warm shawl, for when the cold came.

"You're a good boy," said his mother, as he set out that night. "Keep safe. Nothing in the world is as precious to me as you are."

Under the shining light of the moon, Curdie made his way up the mountain, slipping through the caverns where he worked, edging himself down the snaking passages. And then he crept further and deeper into the heart of the mountain.

Further and deeper still… until, at last, he heard goblin voices. He picked away at some loose stones, very softly, so they wouldn't hear, and made a tiny window into their secret world.

He saw a group of them gathered around a fire in a gloomy cavern. The goblins had stones in their hair, glowing in dull, gorgeous shades in the firelight; two wore spiky, silver crowns.

"It's a meeting – with the goblin King and Queen," Curdie thought to himself, hardly believing his luck.

"Great news," said the King. "The tunnels we've been digging are now directly underneath the castle. We'll break through early tomorrow morning and invade!"

"That *will* be fun," crowed the Queen.

Curdie crept closer, to hear better. But to his horror, the rocks beneath his feet began to wobble, then collapsed beneath him, pebbles scattering everywhere. Curdie toppled head over heels, through the loose stones, landing right at the goblins' feet.

"What have we here?" shouted the King. "A human spy!"

"Lock him up," squealed the Queen.

"Good idea! Get him!" ordered the King.

Hundreds of goblin guards surged into the cave, shouting and waving their fists at Curdie. He began stamping on their feet, as fast as he could, but there were far too many for him to reach them all.

The goblins overpowered him, and threw him into a hole beside the cave. Curdie could hear them whispering, but however hard he listened, he couldn't catch their words. Then, as a group of them dragged a stone slab across the opening, he heard a wisp of their conversation…

"… only one thing worse than stamping feet, and that's the power of rhyme…"

Just as Curdie was puzzling over this, the last

glimmer of light disappeared. Now he was all alone in the dark, knowing the castle was in danger, and he couldn't do a thing to help…

In her bedroom painted with stars, Esme woke suddenly, to see her ring glittering brightly in the darkness. "What's this?" she wondered. "Does Grandmother need me?"

She rose from her bed, feeling the gossamer line of thread. To her surprise, it didn't lead her deeper into the castle, but outside, into the garden, and up the mountainside. She was cold in the chill night air, but she didn't care. She knew she had to follow the magic thread, just as she'd promised her grandmother.

The mountain path became steeper, till it was hardly a path at all, just a stumbling, uneven drift of stones.

Esme was puzzled, but she kept her hand on the thread. On and up she went, till it took her to a small hole in the side of the mountain, not much bigger than a badger's. She slipped inside, and found she was in a cave, echoing with drips of water. Esme felt very far from her own safe castle.

The thread led her through the cave, down dark passages, so low she had to crouch, then crawl on her hands and knees.

Her ring reassured her, because in the darkness it was glowing like a friendly little fire. Now the thread took her to a heap of stones by a wall, and then, bewilderingly, it stopped.

"What shall I do?" Esme wondered, feeling her courage slipping away. "Should I go home?"

But when she turned back, she couldn't feel the thread. It was telling her to go through the stones.

"Grandmother must have brought me here for a reason," she said. "I'll have to keep trying."

She began to undo the pile of stones, even as they slipped through her fingers, cutting her with their jagged edges. At last, the pile was at an end, and now only one great stone was left.

"Who's there?" said a voice.

"Oh Curdie!" Esme called back. "Is that you? It's me, Esme."

"I've been trapped in this cave by the goblins," Curdie called back. "What are you doing here?"

"My grandmother sent me. I must be here to rescue you. I've undone all the stones, and if you push the big one now, I think it will move."

Curdie gave it a great shove and it fell with a crash. Out he stepped, blinking with amazement.

"Let's go," Esme said.

"Easier said than done," replied Curdie. "I'm a miner, and even I don't know all these passages."

"We'll just follow the thread," said Esme.

"What do you mean?" asked Curdie.

"It's a gift from my grandmother. She lives in a turret in the castle, in a room with fire-roses and a lamp that shines like the moon. She gave me this ring with an invisible thread. She said I should trust it. I'm sure it will lead us out of here."

Esme could tell from Curdie's expression that he didn't believe a word. But he followed her all the same, amazed at the way she led him through the darkness, winding this way and that through the narrow passages, till at last they emerged on the mountainside, just as the sun was rising.

"Do you believe me now, Curdie?" asked Esme.

"I don't know," said Curdie, scratching his head. "But we have to hurry. I overhead the goblins' plans while I was down the mines and they're going to invade the castle. We have to warn everyone."

Hand in hand, they rushed back to the castle, but by the time they pushed through the huge front door, it was already too late. Everywhere was awash with goblins. They swarmed from every nook and cranny, bursting out of cupboards, squirming up from cracks in the floorboards and leaping through the windows.

In the Great Hall, the goblin King and Queen sat on thrones, grinning gleefully, while the castle servants huddled in the corner, shivering with fear.

"Stamp on their feet!" cried Curdie. "The goblins hate that!"

He and Lootie sprang into action, stamping as hard and fast as they could. Curdie was like a small whirlwind, and away scattered the goblins.

Before long, they were all fleeing – howling,

In the Great Hall, the goblin King and Queen sat on thrones,
grinning gleefully…

limping, shrieking, trying to hold their feet in their hands. At last, the hall was empty…

"Wait!" cried Lootie. "Where's the Princess?"

"The goblin King and Queen took her!" said a breathless servant, running in from outside. "I tried to stop them, but they wore stone shoes on their feet, so no matter how hard I stamped, it didn't make any difference."

"I'll find the Princess," said Curdie, rushing out the door. But then he stopped for a moment, wondering which way to go. Above his head, he saw a light, round and shining like the moon, and he thought of what Esme had told him about her grandmother. He reached out, and to his amazement, he felt a thread between his fingers, as light and strong as spider silk.

He followed the thread, back up the mountain, and there was Esme, being dragged away by the goblin King and Queen. Suddenly he remembered the words he'd overheard in the cave. "Rhyme!" he called out to Esme. "They hate rhyme!"

Curdie desperately tried to think of a rhyme himself, but his mind had gone blank. He started running towards Esme, but she was far ahead by now. How would he ever find her in the mountain?

Esme watched him running. She knew he'd never reach her in time. "I'm a princess," she told herself, bravely. "I have to help myself." And despite her rising panic, she began to chant – any rhyme that came into her head…

"Hush! Scush! Scurry!
Go in a hurry!
Gobble, gobble, goblin!
There you go a wobblin',
Hobble, hobble, hobblin',
Hob-bob-goblin!"

The goblin King and Queen loosed their hold and covered their ears. "No!" they shouted. "Stop that! Stop!"

"Keep going!" called Curdie,

still running up the mountain path.

More and more words tripped off Esme's tongue. She felt their power, their magic… the way they fizzed and crackled through the air.

"One, two – pick a shoe!
Three, four – shut the door.
Five, six – there's a fix!
Seven, eight – hold it straight.
Nine, ten – go again!"

The goblin King and Queen could bear it no longer. They raced away from Esme, howling, as sure as if their tender feet had been struck.

"You did it, Esme!" cried Curdie, reaching her at last. "You did it!"

They watched the goblins disappear back into the darkness of the mountain. When they had gone, Curdie saw a vision he would never forget. A tall old lady dressed in silver, radiant as a star.

"Well done," she said to both of them, smiling. "You showed true courage today. And you won't have to worry about the goblins ever again."

"We won't?" asked Curdie.

"From now on, you'll find that both their heads and their hearts will become softer, even as their feet grow harder. Now go quickly," she went on. "The King has returned. He is waiting for Esme in the Great Hall."

Curdie found himself giving a little bow, for there was something about the old lady, perhaps it was the way she looked at him, or the kindness in her voice, that made him feel very humble.

Esme hugged her grandmother tight. "Thank you," she said, "for everything."

Then Curdie and Esme hurried on towards the castle. "I'm so glad you saw my grandmother too," said Esme. "And that you believe in her."

Curdie took one last look over his shoulder, but

as he did so the vision of the old lady began to flicker and fade. A moment later, all he saw was a faint shimmer, and then a dove, flying away in the last of the dawn light.

When they reached the castle, a great cheer went up. The King, his face fraught, rushed towards Esme, and caught her up in his arms.

"I was coming back to you," he said, "and then I saw goblins, fleeing the castle, and I feared they'd captured you…"

"I'm safe now," said Esme. "Curdie helped me, and Grandmother."

For a moment, the King couldn't speak for joy, or take in anything else but his own Esme, clasped in his embrace.

"I'm going to bring you back to the city," said the King. "I don't want to be without you again." Then he turned to Curdie. "How can I reward you? Would you like to come with us? Anything you ask for, it's yours."

But Curdie shook his head. "I must stay with my parents," he said. "But I would like a shawl, for my mother, to keep her warm when winter comes."

"Is that all?" asked the King. "Of course you shall have one, the finest ever made. But if you ever need anything else, you only have to ask."

The next day, the King took Esme away on his horse. Lootie was to follow later, in a carriage. Esme hugged her goodbye, and then the servants. Her last hug was for Curdie.

"It's not goodbye, Curdie," she promised him as they rode away. "I won't let it be."

And one day, the Princess and Curdie did meet again, but that, as they say, is another story…

This story was first published as a book in 1863.
It was originally called The Water-Babies,
A Fairy Tale for a Land Baby.

The Water Babies

*L*ong ago, when children were sent up chimneys to clean them, there was a little chimney sweep named Tom. He belonged to Mr. Grimes, a cruel master who made Tom climb chimneys even when he didn't want to, when his knees and elbows were rubbed raw and he trembled from his fear of the dark.

Worse still, Tom had never been given any kindness or love, or had the chance to show it to others. Instead, he was learning to be as tough as Mr. Grimes. He had no choice, for every day he had to go up the dark, narrow chimneys that scared him.

Sometimes, when Tom wasn't working, he played with the other chimney sweeps and smiled and laughed like any other boy. And sometimes, Tom dreamed… of being all grown-up, a man like Mr. Grimes, and then it would be *his* turn to make boys go up chimneys.

One day, Mr. Grimes took Tom out of the big, grimy city where they lived, and way out over the moors, to sweep the chimneys at a grand house, belonging to a Sir John Harthover. Tom and Mr. Grimes walked over at sunrise, Tom carrying the brushes. He walked barefoot, for he had no shoes.

Tom had never seen the countryside before. He was amazed at the buttercups and daisies and wild raspberries, and a sparkling little stream that bubbled beside the path. He wanted to paddle and play, but Mr. Grimes wouldn't let him.

"Don't waste time, boy. You have a lot of chimneys to sweep today."

A countrywoman was walking just behind them. She, too, was barefoot, with a shabby shawl over her head, but with kind, wise eyes. As Mr. Grimes pulled Tom away from the water, she called out, "Aren't you ashamed of yourself, Grimes?"

"How do you know me?" Mr. Grimes replied, startled at her use of his name.

"I know what I know," she said quietly, looking at him full in the face. "Those who wish to be clean, clean they will be. Those who wish to be foul, foul they will be."

She turned away, and when Mr. Grimes looked for her again on the path, she was nowhere to be seen.

At last they came up a sweeping driveway. Tom gawped when he saw the size of the house.

"We'll begin with the largest chimney," said Mr. Grimes, leading him to the biggest room of all. He pushed Tom towards the fireplace.

Tom took his brushes and began to climb the chimney. Up… up… up he went. But the chimneys were crooked and rambling and all ran into one another, and Tom very soon realized he was lost.

When he came down the chimney again, he knew at once he'd gone the wrong way. He was in a pretty bedroom, and fast asleep in the bed was a girl, about his own age. She looked so peaceful, and happy, and beautiful, Tom couldn't stop staring. Then, for the first time in his life, he saw himself in a mirror.

"Is that really me?" he wondered, peering closer. "But I'm so ragged and dirty, and I'm all covered in soot and smuts."

He turned away from himself. "I shouldn't be here, in this lovely bedroom," he thought. "I don't belong." He tried to sneak back up the chimney, but he tripped against the fire irons, which fell over with a loud clatter.

The girl sat up in bed and screamed.

A moment later, the door burst open and in rushed her nanny. "What is it, Ellie?" she asked.

Ellie, mouth open, soundless now, simply pointed at Tom, frozen to the spot.

The nanny grabbed Tom's arm, but he squirmed away, quick as a flash. He raced down the corridors, out a side door, and he kept running.

"Thief! Thief!" the nanny yelled after him, thinking he'd come to steal. And soon the whole household was chasing him over the moor – Sir John, the nanny, all the servants, Mr. Grimes, some on horseback, others running, dogs too, barking and snapping. On ran Tom.

"I've got to hide," he thought. Down a steep slope he ran, but he tripped on a tree root, and then he was falling, head over heels, tumbling, over and over. When at last he stopped falling, he saw there was a river before him, shining cool and clear.

Tom gazed longingly into the shining water, where every pebble sparkled up at him.

"If I go in, I'll be clean," he thought, "as clean as that girl in the big house."

And before he could think more about it, he was pulling off his shirt and trousers, and dipping his feet in the water. It felt so soft and so inviting that Tom slipped in further. He was floating now in the cool, clear water. He shut his eyes, and in no time at all he was in the most soothing sleep of his life.

When Sir John and the servants and the rest of the household arrived at the river, all they found was a heap of clothes, but no Tom.

They thought he'd been drowned, and they all blamed themselves. Ellie felt dreadful because she'd screamed and set the whole thing off. But Tom wasn't drowned at all. Instead something magical had happened…

He had turned into a water baby.

When Tom opened his eyes again, he was under the water, in a little swimsuit, swimming as he'd never swum before. He was only about four inches long, and he was as clean and lively as a fish. He darted this way and that, gazing at all the wondrous things in the river.

There were water flowers with waving tendrils, and tiny trout. When he bobbed his head above the surface he saw dragonflies with iridescent wings. His mind was full to the brim with the river and the dancing sunlight, and everything that had happened faded from his memory, so it seemed no more than a dream. All he knew was that he was happy and free. If he had one doubt about this new life, this river life, it was that he was lonely, as there were no other creatures like himself.

And this was how Tom lived, day after day, like a long, long summer without end. But then came the day when the sky grew darker and a huge black cloud billowed overhead. Thunder rumbled, louder and louder, and hail fell, as large as pebbles, pelting the river, churning it all to foam. The water rose, till it was full of creatures twisting and turning and rushing in the current. Tom could hear them say, "We must hurry. Down to the sea, down to the sea."

Terrified, Tom clung to the reeds, resisting the force of the river until, in a flash of lightning, he saw three little girls, water babies like himself, floating down the torrent, singing, "Down to the sea."

"Wait for me," cried Tom, but they were gone, though he could hear their voices, sweet and clear, singing their song.

Tom hurried after them, following the flow. He swam past boats, and watermills, on and on, and at last the river began to change, turning over and over, and the water no longer tasted cool and clear, but was laced with salt. It was the tide, of course, and it carried Tom with it, out to sea.

Tom swam with the tide, longing to find the other water babies. And as he went, he felt himself begin to change. He felt stronger, as though his limbs were flexed and dancing.

Far out over the waves, he met an old seal.

"Are you looking for your brothers and sisters?" asked the seal. "I passed them just now."

"I never saw them," said Tom, excited. "Friends at last!" he thought. But in all the great sea, among fish, porpoises and sea snails, he couldn't find them.

"All that way for nothing," he grumbled, and he turned back to the rocks near the shore. But there, finally, he saw one – a water baby just like himself. "A friend!" he cried, swimming over. "Where have you been, all this time? I've been so lonely."

"There are hundreds of us among the rocks," said the other water baby. "I can't think why you've never seen us. Now you can help me with this rock pool. It got ripped apart in the last storm, and I must plant it again, with seaweed and anemones, and make it the prettiest rock garden ever."

They worked away, smoothing the sand around it, and when they'd finished, they were surrounded by dozens of water babies, singing and playing.

"You've come to join us!" they laughed.

They worked away, smoothing the sand around it, and when they'd finished, they were surrounded by dozens of water babies…

Tom had never been so happy. But even as he played with his new-found friends, Tom couldn't resist frightening the crabs, and putting stones into the anemones' mouths, so they were tricked into thinking they were getting their dinner. It wasn't kind of him, but then Tom knew nothing about being kind.

"Careful," warned the other water babies. "Mrs. BeDoneByAsYouDid is coming."

"Why should that matter?" said Tom, in high spirits, and carried on with his teasing.

Mrs. BeDoneByAsYouDid was a fairy, with a fierce face, sharp eyebrows and a great pair of green spectacles. When she arrived, all the water babies lined up and she looked them over. She seemed pleased with them and handed out all sorts of delicious things to eat – sea-toffee, sea-apples,

sea-grapes and lollipops. Tom was getting excited. But when it was his turn to come up, she popped into his mouth a hard, cold pebble.

"That was cruel!" protested Tom.

"And you're a cruel boy. That's what you did to the sea anemones, and as you did, so I must do to you."

"I didn't know it was wrong," said Tom.

"Well, I'm not so cross with you as I would be if you did know. It's my job to punish those who do wrong, especially those who are cruel to children."

Tom suddenly remembered Mr. Grimes.

"Yes, Mr. Grimes, your old master," said Mrs. BeDoneByAsYouDid, who could read thoughts. "But you mustn't worry about him anymore. He'll learn his lesson. Now, tomorrow, you'll meet my sister, Mrs. DoAsYouWouldBeDoneBy, and I expect you'll like her a lot more than me."

Tom gazed up into her all-knowing eyes. He realized she looked just like the woman he'd met on the moor, who had scolded Mr. Grimes for not letting Tom play in the water. Quickly, he resolved never to tease animals again.

Tomorrow arrived and with it came Mrs. DoAsYouWouldBeDoneBy. All the water babies began clapping their hands, and Tom could understand why. For here was the loveliest, most motherly fairy you ever did see, with the tenderest smile and the kindest eyes and the softest face. She gathered up armfuls of water babies, Tom too, and cuddled him. He'd never in his whole life known anything like this, and it made him so happy, he thought he'd explode with love.

"I must go now," she said, after she'd been with the water babies for a good while. "Will you be a good boy, and be kind to the sea creatures, Tom?" she asked.

"I promise," said Tom. "Will you come back to me again?"

"I'll always come back," she promised.

Tom tried to be kind and good, always, after that, but being good *all* the time was very hard. Tom had been watching Mrs. BeDoneByAsYouDid whenever she came to give the water babies their treats and lollipops, and now he had discovered where she kept them – in a beautiful mother-of-pearl cupboard hidden in the rocks.

At first, Tom was only going to *look* at the lollipops, then it seemed a pity not to *touch* them, and then seeing as he was touching them, it was only natural to *eat* one. Just one. Except he couldn't help gobbling up lots of them, they were so delicious.

Mrs. BeDoneByAsYouDid knew what he was up to, because she knew everything. But she didn't say a word. The next time she came, Tom felt very afraid, in case there were no lollipops, and that he should be found out, but to his surprise, there were just as many as ever.

Mrs. BeDoneByAsYouDid looked him full in the face, and Tom shook, but she gave him a lollipop and Tom was relieved that he hadn't been found out. But when he put the lollipop in his mouth, he hated the taste of it. Instead of being deliciously sweet, it tasted slimy and rotten and he had no pleasure in it at all.

The next week, when Mrs. BeDoneByAsYouDid came again, she looked Tom full in the face once more, her own full of sorrow. Still, Tom didn't say a word, but took the lollipop, even though it tasted just as bad as before.

"Perhaps I won't ever be found out?" he thought. But when Mrs. DoAsYouWouldBeDoneBy came and Tom wanted to be cuddled by her like all the rest, she turned to him and said, "I can't cuddle you, Tom, because you're covered in prickles."

Tom looked at himself, and he saw he was as prickly as a hedgehog.

All week, Tom felt miserable. No one wanted to play with him, so he sat in a corner on his own. And when Mrs. BeDoneByAsYouDid came back, and offered him his lollipop, looking at him more seriously than ever, he burst into tears.

"I don't want any!" he said, and told her everything that had happened. Then he waited, horribly frightened that she would punish him. But instead, she hugged him and kissed him and told him that she forgave him.

"I expect you've never had enough to eat," she said, "or been taught how important it is to share – but I think you're beginning to learn that for yourself."

Tom thought about the horrid-tasting lollipops and realized it was his guilt that had made them taste that way. He nodded.

"Now can you take away my prickles?" he asked.

"Only you can do that," she replied. "But I'll find someone to help you."

Tom was scared at first, expecting a strict teacher, but instead she brought him a little girl. Tom recognized her. It was Ellie.

She didn't recognize him, but she did begin teaching him. She told him stories about being kind and good and happy, how important it was not to steal or be greedy, and gradually every prickle disappeared.

Now Ellie recognized him.

"You're the chimney sweep who came into my room," she exclaimed.

They talked and talked, and soon were the best of friends.

"What are you doing down here, under the sea?" asked Tom. "Did you fall into the water, too?"

"No," said Ellie. "A fairy came to me one night, as I was drifting to sleep, and said there was someone who needed my help. When I agreed to come, she brushed my eyelids with sea grass, and sprinkled me with sea lavender, and the next thing I knew I was here with you. But now that you're cured of your prickles, it's time for me to go home."

Tom was desperately sorry to see Ellie leave, and longed to go with her. But Mrs. DoAsYouWouldBeDoneBy told him there was one more thing he needed to do.

"What's that?" asked Tom.

"You've been helped, so now it's your turn to help someone else."

"Who?" asked Tom.

"Mr. Grimes," she replied. "We have brought him to the world beneath the sea, too, although he's not a water baby, like you. Now you're cured of your prickles, you must see what you can do to help him."

"But he'll turn me back into a chimney sweep again," cried Tom.

"He can't. No one can turn a water baby into a chimney sweep."

"I think this'll be the hardest thing I've ever done," whispered Tom. "But I'll go if I must."

So Tom set out on his journey, determined to show Mrs. DoAsYouWouldBeDoneBy how brave he could be. He swam through secret haunts of water unknown to humans, far beyond whales and dolphins, ten thousand fathoms deep below roaming sharks. He rose up again, past walls of ice and curtains of mist, amid puffins and geese and storm petrels, all around the world, till at last he came down to a land beneath the sea that consisted entirely of chimneys. And there, guarding them, was a porter, with a deep gruff voice who told Tom that Grimes, the master chimney sweep, was up chimney 345.

"If you want to talk to him, you'd better go up on the roof."

So Tom climbed up, and over the great piles of coal lying around. He found chimney 345. And

out of the top of it was Mr. Grimes
himself, stuck fast in the chimney,
so miserable-looking that Tom could
hardly bear it.

"Ah," said Mr. Grimes. "It's Tom.
I suppose you've come to laugh
at me."

"No," said Tom. "I've come to
help you."

"No one can help me," said Mr.
Grimes. "Did I ask to be brought
here, to this chimney prison? Did I
ask to have lighted straw put under
me to make me climb up? Did I ask
to get stuck in this chimney?"

345

"No," said a voice behind. "And nor did Tom, when you did just the same to him."

It was Mrs. BeDoneByAsYouDid.

Tom turned to her. "Don't worry about me," he said. "That's all in the past. Can't I try to help Mr. Grimes, by undoing some of these bricks, so he can move his arms?"

"You can try," said the fairy.

So Tom tried, but the bricks wouldn't come away. Then it began to hail. Great lumps of ice hit Mr. Grimes's head and hurt him.

"These are the tears of everyone you've ever hurt, but your cold heart freezes them to ice," said Mrs. BeDoneByAsYouDid.

Then Mr. Grimes began to cry. "I'm sorry for everything I did. I wish I could go back and start again, but now it's too late."

"Oh, Mr. Grimes!" said Mrs. BeDoneByAsYouDid. "It's never too late."

Now she looked so like her sister, Mrs. DoAsYouWouldBeDoneBy, and the wise woman on the moor, that they seemed all like the same person, with a strong, kind face and clear, wise eyes. And as Mr. Grimes kept on crying great blubbery tears, they streamed down his face in rivers, and washed all the cement away from the chimney bricks, so the chimney crumbled.

"Don't you remember what I said to you on the moor?" asked Mrs. BeDoneByAsYouDid. "*Those who wish to be clean, clean they shall be?* You got your wish, and now you have another chance. Go. And be good."

Mr. Grimes stepped out of the crumbling chimney and Mrs. BeDoneByAsYouDid led him away, to begin his life again.

"Wait here, Tom," she said. "I shall be back soon."

When she came back, she spoke to Tom very seriously. "You've been kind and you've been brave. You have come to the end of your journey, and you have a choice. Would you like to be a water baby forever, or would you like to be a boy again?"

"I'd like to be a boy," said Tom. "But I don't want to be a chimney sweep."

"You never will, I promise you. I'll take you back, but not the long way, the way you got here, swimming. Hold my hand, and we'll fly."

Flying upwards through water was the strangest sensation, Tom found. Light as a dandelion clock, he soared, and then, little by little, his limbs grew heavier and the water felt like a weighty cloak. When he reached the surface of the water, the fairy had gone. He was choking and spluttering, clinging on to a hand, gazing up at a kind face.

It was Sir John Harthover, whose chimneys Tom had swept such a long time ago, it seemed.

"You're not drowned, thank goodness, little lad," cried Sir John, patting Tom's back to calm the last of his coughs. "We've looked for you everywhere. We've been so worried. Ellie especially."

"Ellie…?" said Tom wonderingly, rubbing his watery eyes.

"My little girl. You came down her chimney, into her bedroom. Do you remember?"

Tom remembered. And glimpses of what had happened next, running away, falling into the river, being a water baby… all these memories hovered for a second and then slipped away. They vanished, like fish darting from the river to the vast open sea. And then he wondered if it had all been a dream. And as he wondered, he forgot more.

"Come home with me," Sir John was saying.

"Ellie would love that. We can give you a home. You can live here, grow up happily, with no one to make you climb chimneys ever again. We owe you that, for having chased you away to nearly drown in the river. Will you come, Tom?"

"Yes," said Tom. "I'd like that."

So the story ends… Tom never did remember being a water baby. And he forgot he'd met Ellie under the sea. But that didn't matter. They were the best of friends. What did matter was that all his life, he had flashes of remembering something, like sparks of sunlight dancing on water… a journey, and trying hard, and being rewarded. And all his life, Tom was happy in himself, and just as importantly, he thought about how he could help others to be happy too. Mrs. DoAsYouWouldBeDoneBy and Mrs. BeDoneByAsYouDid would have been proud of him.

This tale is based on a story called Amelia and the Dwarfs, *first published in 1870.*

Amelia
and the
Elves

There was once a couple who had one daughter, Amelia, who was strong-willed and clever but very, very spoiled.

Every time she passed a toyshop, her mother bought her something. She had her own pet dog, a bulldog, whom she loved, but couldn't resist teasing. She'd hold out a bun, and just as he'd be about to eat it, she'd snatch it away.

Amelia never had to do anything for herself.
She had a nanny who kept her clothes clean and
tidy. But Amelia was *so* naughty, that she rolled
in the mud on purpose, and would tear her skirt
when climbing trees. Then her poor nanny had
to wash and iron everything and her old eyes
were worn out, darning the great jagged rips
by candlelight.

Other families would dread Amelia's visits.
She'd pick up valuable pieces of
china, twiddling them on her
fingertips till they fell on
the floor and smashed to
smithereens.

When Amelia's parents
gave dinner parties,
Amelia always stayed up,
interrupting everyone in her
loud voice, till they all wished
she'd go to bed. But her mother only said, "Isn't
Amelia the sweetest child you ever saw!"

And mealtimes! The amount of food Amelia wasted! If she didn't like her chicken and mashed potatoes, her mother would coax her with a little roast beef and peas. And when she'd played with that, she'd sigh and try raspberry tart and cream, and when *that* wasn't finished, she was given cheese and biscuits. "Amelia," sighed her mother, "has a very *delicate* appetite."

What Amelia loved most of all, however, were long summer evenings. She'd gaze out of her bedroom window at the fields of golden hay. Then, come harvest time, she'd run into the fields, getting in everyone's way. The haymakers wished she'd go indoors, but her mother said, "My poor darling child *must* have a little treat sometimes."

One summer evening, Amelia peeped out of her window and saw that four hay bales had been left in the field, each with a deep shadow at its side.

"I must go and jump on the hay bales!" she cried. "I want to have some fun."

"No," Nanny replied. "The field is wet with dew.

And it's a moonlit night. Who knows what you might see? Besides, there's been a magpie hopping about all day. That's a sure sign of bad luck."

"Who cares?" said Amelia, stamping her foot. "I'll do what I want."

Later, when the moon shone silvery gold, and no one was looking, Amelia slipped out to the hayfield. She was alone, yet with every step, she felt she was not. Then she saw a little man dressed in green, with green shoes that had long points at their tips. He had bright, darting eyes, and quick-moving hands, with long nails and twirling fingers.

"That's an elf!" Amelia said to herself, amazed. She hid, kneeling in the shadow of a hay bale, and watched.

More elves appeared, like magic. And more and more. They were climbing out of the hay bales, and suddenly the whole hayfield was swarming with little men dressed in all shades of green; light green, bright green, grass green, fir green, forest green, blue green, yellow green, dark green.

They darted between the hay bales, in and out
of the shadows, till the field was alive with bright
eyes gleaming and lithe limbs running, shining like
sticks of emeralds in the moonlight. A dozen tiny
voices cried, "Let's dance!"

"No!" said the first elf. "For Amelia is hiding
here! But we'll take her below, and then she will
be ours! And then maybe we'll come back and
dance here!"

Now Amelia was many things, but she wasn't
a coward. She came out of her hiding place and
strode between the elves. "This is my papa's field,"
she told them. "It's not yours to dance in."

"Under the moon, everything belongs to us," said the elf, and he danced around her singing:

All under the sun belongs to men,
And all under the moon to the fairies.
The day is theirs, the night is ours,
Hey ho! for the elves and the fairies.

"And now," he announced, "you're coming with us, Amelia."

"I'm not coming," Amelia retorted, although she couldn't help feeling curious.

"Oh yes you are," said the elf. Then he called out to the others, "I've got Amelia. Bring the changeling!"

"A changeling?" said Amelia. "What's a changeling?"

"You'll see!" laughed the elf.

And she watched as the elves plucked something from the bale of hay, and lifted what seemed to Amelia to be a little girl. It was *exactly* like her, her own face, clothes, hair, everything.

"A changeling is a fairy creature!" said the elf. "But with a sprinkling of spells, we've made it look just like you. Even your parents will take it for Amelia. Now," he said, instructing the other elves, "the father and mother are coming. Lay the changeling down in the field."

And the next moment, Amelia was pushed right inside the hay bale. The hay smelled strong and sweet. Its scent swept over her, making her limbs feel full and heavy. As if in a dream, she peered out through the hay, watching as her parents and her nanny picked up the changeling child who looked just like her.

The changeling moaned, and now the elves rubbed Amelia's eyes with magic ointment.

At once, she saw the changeling was nothing but a hairy imp with a twisted, sneering face.

"Send Amelia below," ordered the first elf.

The ground beneath the hay bale opened, and, with a *whoosh!* Amelia slipped down a dark tunnel. She was too scared to be angry, and too angry to be scared. She tumbled and turned and fell, unhurt, onto an underground heath. There were no trees, no houses, but flowers everywhere, glowing softly, with the same muted light as the moon.

The air was dreamy, with a quiet wind that swayed the flowers and carried their gentle perfumes. Over the heath lay the cool, rising light of early dawn. It would all have been beautiful, but every few paces

were blocked by piles of clothes. Torn, wet, muddy, dirty, sandy. Amelia recognized them. They were hers.

"Wash them," said the elf.

"I can't," said Amelia. "Tell Nanny. It's her job."

"You must," said the elf. "We can't dance down here because your dirty clothes are in our way. She'll help you clean up all the mess you've made."

He pointed with his long sharp shoe to an old woman who sat quietly by a fire. She seemed to be a real woman, not a fairy.

"Now, get to work," ordered the elf. Without a word, the woman showed her a wash-tub, and jugs of water. There was a cauldron, so she could heat the water over the fire, and bars of soap.

Soon, Amelia's back ached with stooping over the wash-tub. Her hands and arms grew wrinkled from the water, and sore with rubbing. The elves came back to check on her, and when she was slow, they ordered her to hurry.

The old woman taught her what to do. At first she was sharp and cross, but when Amelia tried her best, she was kind, and even helped her. When Amelia grew hungry, she asked one of the elves for food.

"Certainly," he said, and led her to a pile of meat and pies and treats that Amelia had once wasted.

"I can't eat these cold scraps," said Amelia.

"Then why did you say you were hungry?" asked the elf.

Amelia was so famished that she ate some cold rice pudding and a pie crust. How delicious they tasted! After a time, she asked if she could heat up some of the scraps over the fire.

"You can do what you want to make yourself comfortable," said the old woman, "as long as you do it yourself."

At last all her dresses were clean, and now they had to be mended. Amelia looked at the great jagged tears where she'd put her foot through her skirts, and wept. She'd always hated sewing, but by now, she'd grown so well-behaved that the old woman pitied her. She helped Amelia, while Amelia cooked for them both. There was no night and no day down on the heath, so when they were tired, they slept whenever they wanted by the fire. Amelia made up stories to amuse the old woman, and tried to remember for her all the poetry she'd once learned.

The old woman told her that she'd been with the elves for a long, long time. "We have no way of measuring time underground, no sun, no moon, so I don't know how many days and weeks and years I've been here," she said.

Her words filled Amelia with despair. "Do you think they'll ever let me go home?" she asked.

"Not now," said the old woman. "When you first came, you were such a selfish, useless little miss that no one would want you longer than was necessary. But now you're a willing, handy little thing. It won't be so bad. They'll make a pet of you, you'll see."

"I want my parents!" cried Amelia. "And that changeling – she'll want her own people, surely?"

"After a time, the changeling will seem ill. She'll slowly fade away, and then she'll take possession of the first black cat she sees, and in that shape she'll leave the house and come home," said the old woman.

"Then my parents will never look for me!" cried Amelia.

Seeing her tears and distress, the old woman offered to give her some advice. "Can you dance?" she asked.

"Yes," Amelia replied. "I can dance."

"Then you must dance whenever you can," said the old woman. "The elves love dancing."

"And what will happen when I dance?"

"If you're lucky, the elves will take you up to dance with them in the fields, above ground."

"But I couldn't get away," said Amelia. "They'd run after me…"

"Your only chance is this," the old woman went on. "Look for a four-leafed clover. If you find one, hold it up and wish to be at home. But for now, you must seem happy, so they think you've forgotten about your home. And don't forget, dance!"

"What about you?" asked Amelia. "Can I do anything to help you get home? You've been so kind to me."

"No," the old woman replied with a smile. "I'm used to this. The light and noise of the world would be too much for me. I am happy here now, in this quiet world. But I wish you well, and remember – dance!"

The woman stopped talking as an elf came by,

and Amelia immediately began to balance on one
leg on a pointed foot, and twirl in a pirouette.

"Ho, ho!" said the elf. "So
you can dance?"

"When I am happy,
I can," said Amelia,
sinking into a
graceful curtsy.

"What are you
pleased about?"
the elf snapped
suspiciously.

"The dresses
are washed and
mended."

"Then away
with them!" cried the
elf. "We don't want them cluttering
us here! They can go back into the world."

Several young elves threw them into baskets
and kicked them up. Amelia didn't see how they

went above the ground, for some other elves led her to another part of the heath. This was a rockier area than before, covered in granite boulders. Some were used as seats and tables and some for anvils and workshops. In the hollow of one boulder a fire burned, like a small forge for twisting iron. Laid out on other rocks, Amelia saw all the china she'd broken throughout her life.

An elf was waiting for her. He was dressed in spring green, and looked at her with scorn. "If you're Amelia, you should be ashamed of yourself," he said.

"I am," said Amelia. "I'd like to mend these things, if I can."

"Well, you can't say more than that," said the elf. "I'll show you how."

Amelia fumblingly tried to copy him as he showed her how to mend them. When he let her rest for a moment, she immediately held out her skirts and began her prettiest dance.

"Fa, la, fa!" sang the elf. "Charming! I'm a good

dancer myself. Watch me!"

He bounded with a hop and a skip, turned a somersault, and ended sitting cross-legged on a large boulder.

"Good, wasn't it?" he said.

"Wonderful," Amelia replied.

"Now it's your turn again," said the elf.

But Amelia cunningly replied, "I must work."

"Pshaw!" said the elf. "I'll do it for you. Now dance again."

"Do you know this?" she asked, dancing a few steps of a polka. "I promise I'll teach you if you mend everything."

He was a tall elf, nearly the same height as Amelia, and a good dancing partner. He learned the steps as soon as she showed him. Together they whirled in and out of the boulders, around and around. Between the stones and their steps they made a pattern, and in all the dimness of the heath the dance was the brightest thing in it.

"Now I'll mend all the rest of the china," said

*Together they whirled in and out of the boulders,
around and around.*

the elf, and did so, quickly. It wasn't kicked up into the world like Amelia's clothes. The elf said it would break on the way, and so it was kept underground.

Then he took her a new part of the heath. It had soft, bright moss, shimmering yellow and green, and was covered with pieces of broken thread.

"These are the broken threads of all the conversations you interrupted," he said. "It's too dangerous to dance here, with all those threads twisting around our ankles, but you can't think how wonderful the moss is to dance on." He left her alone. She began to pick up the broken threads of conversation, but it was weary work. Her back ached. After a while, the elf returned with a violin. He lifted it to his chin and began to play.

"Dance!" he called.

"I don't think I can!"

"Then listen!"

He played faster and faster, and, as he played, all the threads danced themselves into three enormous heaps.

"And now for our dance," he smiled. "Our polka! Try this mossy floor, Amelia. I swear you will spin as never before."

Amelia danced better than ever, and the elf was in raptures. When they'd finished dancing, she tossed the threads into three baskets, and a troop of young elves came to carry them away.

"Where shall we kick these?" asked one.

"To the four winds of heaven," replied the dancer elf. "Few drawing room conversations are worth keeping. They're not like precious china."

Amelia's tasks were ended, but no one said anything about her going home. The elves were now all very kind. Evidently, they meant to keep her.

Amelia cooked delicious meals for them and

danced with them, but her heart ached for home, and when she was alone, she cried for her mother and her father. Then one day she overheard the elves talking.

"The moon is full tonight. Let's take Amelia up to the hayfield and dance."

"Is it safe? What happens if she's seen?"

"I'll make her a hat of enchanter's nightshade, so she'll look like a will-o'-the-wisp bobbing up and down," said the dancer elf. "I want to dance with her above ground, in the field in the moonlight. It's a different air from our heath."

"So be it."

Amelia wore her white-flowered hat and went with them. She danced with the elf and their shadows danced with them. As the moon sank, the shadows lengthened and the elf smiled.

"When one sees how big one's shadow is," he remarked, "one knows one's true worth."

The field was just by Amelia's house. Her father, watching by the sickbed of the changeling in Amelia's bedroom, looked out of the window.

"Lovely moonlight…" he murmured, "and there's a will-o'-the-wisp."

That night, Amelia found no four-leafed clover, and at dawn they went underground.

The following night they danced on a hill, and again, no clover plant did Amelia see.

The third night, they danced in the hayfield once more. Their green clothes glimmered in the silvery light, as they leaped and skipped and twirled, and Amelia danced with them all. Their pointed shoes met like the spokes of a wheel, and then kicked out like spikes.

"Ho, ho, ho!" laughed the elves.

"Fa, la, fa!" sang the dancer elf.

"Ha, ha, ha!" laughed Amelia, for she'd found a four-leafed clover. She held it up and cried from her very heart, "I want to go home!"

The elves roared a hideous cry of

disappointment, and at that moment the changeling came tumbling head over heels into their midst, crying, "Oh, the pills and medicines! Oh, the lotions and potions! Oh, the poultices and plasters! Humans may well be short-lived."

And Amelia found herself in her very own bed.

By her bed was a table filled with medicine bottles, and she smiled to think of everything the changeling must have swallowed. Her mother was sitting by her, tears trickling down her cheeks. She looked so worn and thin that Amelia felt her pain.

"Mamma!"

Her voice was so unlike her old imperious snarl that her mother hardly recognized it. Amelia tried to tell her story, but no one believed her.

Her parents thought it was all her illness, and that her poor brain was wandering. Only one creature seemed to know the truth, and that was her bulldog.

When her parents had brought the changeling home, the bulldog had wanted to attack it. He was so wild that they tied him up in the stable. He sat there, day after day, howling. Amelia's nanny said that made her give up hope, and she thought Amelia would die. "For they say a howling dog is a sign of death."

But as soon as Amelia returned, the bulldog came tearing into her bedroom, dragging his chain behind him, nearly choked by his desperate efforts to break it. He jumped onto Amelia's bed, wagging his tail, and there he stayed, watching over Amelia like the chief nurse. And when she told him her story, she could see he believed every word.

So in spite of, or perhaps because of the past, Amelia grew up gentle yet bold, and considerate for others. She was always kind, and unusually clever, as those who have been with the elves are always said to be.

This fairy tale is set in
England, and was
written over a
hundred years ago.

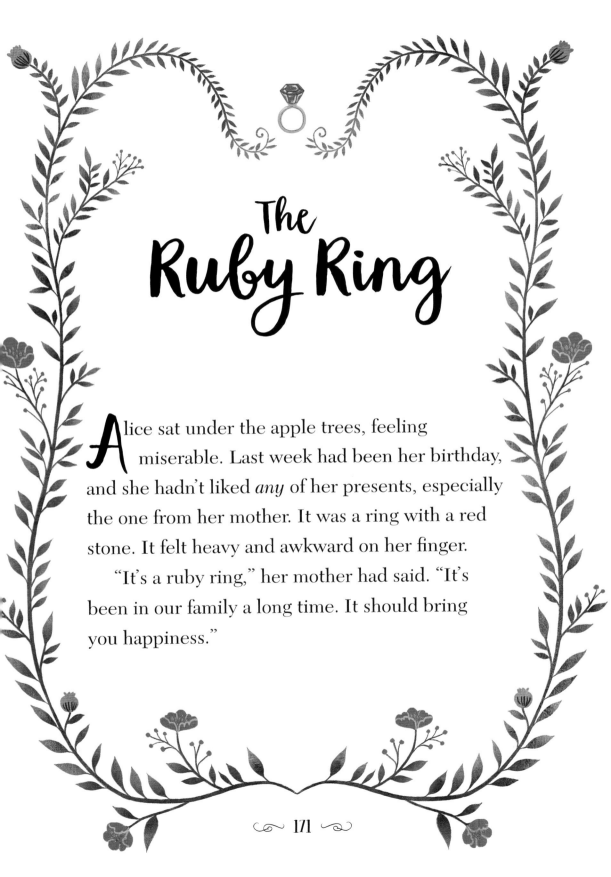

The Ruby Ring

Alice sat under the apple trees, feeling miserable. Last week had been her birthday, and she hadn't liked *any* of her presents, especially the one from her mother. It was a ring with a red stone. It felt heavy and awkward on her finger.

"It's a ruby ring," her mother had said. "It's been in our family a long time. It should bring you happiness."

And now Alice was staying with her Aunt Judy, in the countryside, which made her crosser than ever. She knew why her mother had sent her. It was because she was being "difficult" at home, always arguing with her brother and sister.

"I don't fit into this family," Alice had said.

"Maybe it's being the middle child," her mother had replied, giving her a hug. "Your Aunt Judy was the same."

Alice couldn't imagine her aunt being the same as her. Aunt Judy was always smiling, even when there was nothing to smile about.

Alice didn't know *what* it was that made her feel miserable and prickly… She just knew that she wished her life was different.

"Perhaps if I wasn't me," she thought, "if I could be someone else, then my life would be better."

A robin pecked at the earth nearby, then looked up at her with his bright round eyes. As he did so, her ring blazed in the sunlight.

"Lucky robin," whispered Alice. "You can fly

anywhere you like…"

Just then, an old cart came rattling down the lane beside the orchard. In the back sat a family, all chatting together. Alice saw at once that they were wood folk. Aunt Judy had told her about them – how they lived in the forest, in log cabins thatched with moss, and sold their wares in town on market days.

One of the family was a young girl, about her own age, with a pretty scarf over her hair, and laughing eyes. She leaned out and waved at Alice.

"I'd like to be one of the wood folk," thought Alice, waving back.

She read her book for a while, then got up to go. But as she gathered her things, she realized her ruby ring was gone. "Mother will be furious," she thought, searching for it under the trees, but it was nowhere to be found.

"Here's your ring," said a voice. And there, before her, was an old woman in a red cloak, with the ring, sparkling on her outstretched hand.

"How did you know it was mine?"

"I know a lot of things," said the old woman. "I know you don't like your life."

Alice stared. "You're right. I hate being me."

"Who would you like to be?"

"One of the wood folk," said Alice immediately. "Like the little girl in the cart, so I can live in the forest in a mossy cabin. Or a robin, so I could fly."

"You wish to stop being yourself?"

"Yes," Alice replied, without a moment's doubt.

"Never decide in a hurry," said the old woman. "Think it over, and meet me tomorrow an hour before sunset…"

Later, in bed, Alice kept thinking of the old woman. Was she magic? Was she a witch? Her dreams that night were of robins in red cloaks singing, *"Tomorrow, tomorrow, an hour before sunset."*

The next day, Alice spent the morning helping Aunt Judy with her shopping. In the afternoon, she was sent outside again. She stomped into the orchard and tried to read her book under the apple trees, but soon felt bored. Looking up, she saw the sun was getting low in the sky.

"It must be an hour before sunset," she thought.

Just then, she saw a flicker of something red between the trees. She stared, and there, unmistakably, was the old woman from yesterday.

"You're surprised?" asked the old woman. "This is the time we agreed. Have you decided?"

Alice felt a rush of excitement. "I want to be like that little girl – one of the wood folk."

"Show me your right hand," said the old woman.

Alice held it out.

"Tonight, after you're in bed, put your ring on the little finger of your left hand," said the old woman. "In the morning, you will see."

"Suppose I get tired of being one of the wood folk?" asked Alice.

"Then turn your ring around three and a half times at night, so the ruby is inside. In the morning, if the ruby has twisted itself back, you will know I have received your message."

And, with that, the old woman disappeared.

That night, Alice followed her instructions. When she woke, her pillow felt lumpy and uncomfortable, and a soft voice said, "Matty, it's time to wake up."

Alice opened her eyes to see a girl with kind

eyes looking down at her.
Alice guessed at once that
she was Matty now, and this
must be Matty's big sister.
Then another voice
called, "Diana!"

"Is that you?"
asked Alice, looking up at her.

"Of course it's me, silly girl," said Diana.

For a moment Alice felt dizzy, and she was glad
when the voice called "Diana!" again, and Diana
hurried away.

Alice looked around. She was in a little room
with a curtain for a door. Through the window,
she could see trees all around, with a green light
streaming through their branches.

Then Alice looked at herself. She was wearing
a knitted shawl and a dress with patches. She
gave a shiver of surprise. It was so strange to be in
someone else's clothes.

Diana put her face back through the curtain.

"Now get up, Matty. Everyone's wondering why you're late."

Alice put on a pair of clogs, next to the bed, then hurried outside, where the family was eating breakfast. One of the boys handed her a porridge bowl and Alice stared at it in horror. It was chipped – and she didn't like the wooden spoon with it.

Then the mother said, "Oh Johnny, you've got no sugar for her," and he went into the hut.

"I want milk," she called after him. "Not sugar."

"Milk!" exclaimed Johnny. "It's not often we get milk, and never for breakfast."

He flung a spoonful of sugar into her bowl. Alice tasted it. It wasn't bad. She ate about half and then held it out to Johnny.

"I do so want a drink of milk," she sighed.

"Something's wrong with you this morning, Matty," said Johnny. "We don't have enough money for milk this week."

Alice thought of home, where there was always milk with never a thought of how much it cost.

"Some folk have more than they want," said Johnny, as if reading her mind. "Just think of the little girl we saw the other day under the apple trees – in her fancy dress. She looked like she had everything money could buy! Still, I'd rather be one of the wood folk," he added, sweeping his arms at all the great green trees.

Before Alice could answer, Diana began collecting up the bowls. "Go and help with the horses, Johnny. And Matty, help wash up."

"Wash up what?" asked Alice.

"The bowls and spoons, of course. You don't think they wash themselves, do you?"

Diana gave her a porridge bowl to scrape out, but she could hardly bear to touch it, it looked so dirty. Diana looked at her in surprise. "You're not yourself this morning, are you? Aren't you feeling well? Never mind, I'll help you."

They got the washing-up done just as Johnny's smiling face peered through the doorway. "Let's give the dogs a run, Matty."

Alice jumped up. "Oh yes! Must I change my shoes?" she asked, looking at the clogs on her feet.

Again, they stared at her. "Change your shoes!" exclaimed Diana. "Where's the others, I'd like to know? You're lucky to have such good ones." Then she added gently, "Do they hurt you? Is there a nail that wants knocking in?"

"No," said Alice meekly. "They don't hurt."

Johnny was already running down the path. He whistled, and in a moment three great dogs raced up to them and they all ran on together.

Alice began to enjoy herself. They ran until they collapsed, out of breath, at the side of the road. Johnny climbed into a field, and came back with beautiful leaves and berries, which he tied into little bunches with pieces of string from his pocket.

"Are they for me?" Alice asked.

"They're for selling, of course," laughed Johnny.

They ran back with the dogs and sat outside the hut again, for now it was lunchtime. Alice didn't like the taste of the food, or the smoky air, and she grew so cross that everyone noticed. They asked if her head ached, and Diana puzzled over the change in her bright, happy little sister.

In the afternoon, it rained. Alice had to darn socks, which she did with a sullen frown. At least Mother had taught her how to do it, she thought, so she didn't look foolish.

"What's the matter with you?" asked Matty's father, looking up from his carving.

"She's been different all day," offered Johnny.

Alice didn't know how to explain. "I wish it wouldn't rain," she said at last.

"It's not like you've never seen rain before," said the father, and everyone roared with laughter.

Alice tried not to burst into tears. "I don't fit in here either," she thought. "I want to go back."

That night, she remembered the old woman's instructions. Three and a half times she turned the ring around. She felt afraid, though. Suppose she got it wrong? Suppose she was Matty forever?

When she woke, the ruby had turned itself around again. "My last day, perhaps," Alice thought, and she decided to please Diana, who'd been so kind to her. So she got up before Diana woke, ready to start the day's chores.

"That's more like you, Mat," Diana said approvingly. "After breakfast, you can take the dogs for a run, so your head doesn't ache again."

This was what Alice wanted. She might see the old woman, if only she could get rid of Johnny. As luck would have it, Johnny had run on ahead with the other boys. And just as she'd hoped, no sooner were they out of sight, than the woman in the red cloak appeared from behind a tree.

"You've sent for me already?"

"It wasn't what I thought," said Alice. "I'm tired of having to do so many chores and wear uncomfortable shoes."

"Well," said the old woman. "What then?"

"I want to be a bird – a robin. I'm sure they're happier than humans."

"As you wish," was the answer. "Do as before."

And then there was no one there, only the glimmer of the red cloak through the trees.

Alice went back to the hut, and for the rest of the day, she tried hard to fit in. "But I'm glad it's the last day," she thought. "And tomorrow, I'll have nothing to do but lovely flying to the tops of the highest trees, without all the bother of being a human."

"What a funny noise," was Alice's first thought when she woke. "Tweet, chirrup, tweet!"

The noise of squeaks was deafening.

She remembered quickly – she was a robin! She was in a nest with three other fledglings. She flapped her wings, and one of the birds said, in a series of chirps, which she found she could understand, "Stop fidgeting. This is the last time we'll get fed."

"What do you mean?" asked Alice.

"Weren't you listening? The old birds told us

yesterday. We can look after ourselves now. We're too big for the nest."

"Where will we sleep tonight?" asked Alice.

The robin sneered a little. "Haven't you worked it out? I'll go to a window, so people will get to know me. Then I'll have food during the winter."

"That's what I'll do," said another fledgling.

"Don't come to my window, or I'll fight you," said the first bird.

"I don't want to go near humans," said Alice. "I want to be free and fly high, and roost in the trees."

"All very well in fine weather," said the sneering bird. "But you'll need shelter in winter. You'll be frozen or starved when the ground's hard and there are no berries or worms."

"Worms… ugh!" said Alice.

"You've often eaten them," laughed the other birds, and just then the two parent birds alighted on the nest. Alice opened her beak, and something was rammed in. She decided she had to take robin life as she found it, and it tasted curiously satisfying.

"Now, goodbye," said the father robin.

The first, sneering robin perched on the edge of the nest, and flew off very confidently. The second and third followed quickly. Then it was Alice's turn.

She knew she could fly. Her tiny robin body had its instincts. But her human-mind was less certain, and she was startled when a shove from the old bird launched her into the air.

With a flap and a flutter on uncertain wings, she reached the ground safely, and found the third robin looking about. "Goodbye," it said. "I don't suppose we'll meet again." Then it hopped away.

Alice felt rather upset. "I thought we'd all be friends and go around together. Maybe I should have been a bird that moves in a flock. Well, at least I can fly." And fly she did. Every swoop and glide was wonderful. She perched on the top of a tall pine tree, and looked around. She let herself sway as a breeze stirred the tree tops.

"I'm free of people at last," she said to herself. "It's nice up here in the trees."

But, after a while, it was rather boring. "I'll look for berries," she decided.

She found a bush, and was pleased to see other robins there too, but two of them set on her and flapped her away. Only when they'd finished eating did she pluck up some berries in her beak. Then she felt rather lonely. "Never mind," she decided. "I'll sing."

She hopped on a branch and began. Her tones were sweet and she carolled on, watching the clouds scud across the sky.

Alice didn't get tired of flying and singing all day, but she still felt lonely. When instinct led her to roost in a branch, she was glad to feel drowsy.

The next day was better. There was the wonderful joy of flying, and looking for berries passed the time, but the hours stretched long.

That afternoon it began to rain. Beneath the leaves, Alice listened to its *drip, drip, drip*, and as night drew in, she decided she couldn't stand it any longer. *I'll starve to death in the winter unless I get fed at some house. If I have to be with people, I might as well be myself again. Or is there something else I could be? I need to talk to the old woman.*

She glanced down at her tiny claw. There was her ring, an almost invisible thread of gold, with the ruby like a speck of flame.

She flicked the ring with her beak and to her relief, it revolved itself, three and a half times. Then

Alice fluffed her
feathers and fell asleep.

She woke in the moonlight
to hear a voice calling her,
and looked down to see
the old woman.

"I'm here!" Alice called
back, flying to meet her.

"So you don't like
bird-life?" asked the
old woman.

"No," said Alice.
"The flying's beautiful, but
the birds aren't friendly."

"What *do* you want?" asked the old woman.

"Something completely different. I love flying
and I want company, but I *don't* want to have to
rely on people. Could I be... a fairy?"

"Are you sure?" said the old woman. "If you stay
a fairy for too long, then you can never go back to
being human."

But Alice wasn't listening. "I want to be a fairy, having fun, dancing and being free."

"Ah," said the old woman. "That is one sort of fairy. *My* kind of fairy is very different."

Alice wondered what she meant, and as she looked at her, the wizened old face changed; the sharp eyes shone with beautiful light. The red cloak disappeared and Alice saw two shining wings.

But only for a moment. Then it was over, and the old woman stood there again. "You can be a fairy," she said, "but the longer you stay, the harder it will be to leave. The human part of you will fade, till there's nothing left. Just remember: never let go of your ring. It's your only way of calling me. Now fly away. You will wake as you wish."

Alice hopped back to her branch, too excited to sleep again. The moonlight lit the leaves, and the twigs looked like black lace against its brilliance. It was beautiful and strange, and the strangeness made her feel dreamy, and in the end sleep came.

When Alice woke, she was lying on soft grass, and wearing the loveliest dress she'd ever seen, all white and silvery till she moved, and then every shade of the rainbow flashed into it.

Next came a flock of fairies, crowding around her. "Welcome," said the first fairy.

"Thank you," said Alice. "It's lovely here."

"Much better than anything you've known. Soon you'll really be one of us," said the fairy.

"My name is Al–" began Alice.

The fairy quickly touched her lip, saying, "Hush. No clumsy names here. We call each other whatever comes into our heads. What does it matter? I'm Moonshine today. Jump up and dance. Come on," urged Moonshine, her wings fluttering.

The Ruby Ring

No words can describe the silkiness of that grass, soft as velvet,
yet bouncy as spring moss.

Alice shook her shoulders and her own wings soared her into the air and onto a lawn, where they began to dance. No words can describe the silkiness of that grass, soft as velvet, yet bouncy as spring moss.

"I like this," Alice said to the fairy next to her.

"That's not surprising. Your world is so ugly. I know; I went there once. You-know-who asked us to get a human child and look after her for a while…"

"Do you mean my old woman?"

The fairy looked terrified. "Hush! You've said the forbidden word! We are *always* young!"

She pulled Alice back into the dance, but Alice wondered. *She didn't like me calling the woman old. I remember reading somewhere that fairies live for hundreds of years and then drop like withered flowers.* She thought of the tall, beautiful, calm winged figure. *My old woman must be a different sort of fairy. Much wiser.*

"Keep dancing," said the fairy. "Don't think!"

But Alice had more questions. "Who was the child you looked after?"

"One of the wood folk. But she was no fun. She just slept all the time, till we took her back. She wasn't like you. She likes being herself."

Then she caught Alice's hands and flew off with her into the bright air, though where the light came from, Alice couldn't understand. There was no sun. It was always exactly the same, no night, no day.

Alice played and flew for hours. The minute one game was over, another began. One was called *rainbow dressing* in which the fairies caught dancing light on a crystal prism and wove the shades into a thousand different hues. Alice was clever at it, and the fairies were pleased.

"You'll soon be a real fairy," they said, "and forget your other life."

"I don't want to forget," said Alice. "I might want to go back sometimes, just to see how everyone is."

"You won't want that for long. Oh, the air's so heavy in the human world, and it's so horrible. I could make you forget, if only you'd let me."

She spoke so coaxingly that Alice was frightened. "What would you do?"

"Just touch your eyes with our poppies. Do let me." Then, glancing down, the fairy gave a shriek.

"Your ring!" she cried. "It makes me feel ill! It's like a little fire. Do take it off, to please me."

Alice nearly did, when she remembered the old woman's words: "*… never let go of your ring. It's your only way of calling me…*" And she managed to distract the fairy by saying, "Show me another of your games."

They played thistledown chase. Then there was another game, then another. The fairies never grew tired, but Alice did. She felt as though she'd done nothing real, nothing that mattered, as if she'd eaten nothing but sweets all day.

They let her sleep. She dreamed that tiny hands were trying to pull off her ring, and she woke to hear laughter and little feet scurrying away.

More games, more flying, more dancing… but Alice was still unsatisfied. She didn't want the fairies to suspect she was getting bored, so she forced herself to seem merry.

"Ah, you're nearly one of us," they approved, but when she was almost asleep, after hours of playing, she heard their voices around her.

"Let's leave her while we fly into the human world. Soon she'll be ours, and then we'll gain fifty years of life!"

When they'd gone, Alice sat up. She remembered an old piece of fairy lore. If fairies can keep a child till it loses its wish for its former life, they gain half a century of existence. Then, all at once, a line of poetry came into her head:

They stole little Bridget for seven years long,
And when she came back, her friends were all gone.

What if she'd been in fairyland for years instead of only a few days? A terrible fear swept over her. Suppose, if she ever did get back, her home was full of strangers, her parents gone, and she was an old woman with wrinkled hands?

She twisted her ring, whispering, "My old woman." She didn't want to wait till morning. She wanted help *now*. And to her amazement, the figure in the red cloak was by her side.

"Please," cried Alice. "Take me home. The fairies only like playing, they don't know about loving people, and *home*. I thought I didn't like being myself, but I can see now… It's much better to be yourself, than it is to pretend to be something else. I want to see my family again. *Please*, let me wake in my own bed!"

"My power is limited," said the old woman. "You must work for yourself now, and the way is hard. Come quickly; the door into the human world is open, for the fairies are going through."

She beckoned for Alice to follow. "Now," said the old woman, pointing upwards. "Follow the fairies. Keep out of sight, and make your own way."

"Will I ever see you again?" asked Alice.

"No. But I shall not forget you. Remember this – love your life and use it well, and have the courage to be yourself."

Alice was going to say goodbye, when she saw the vision she'd seen before – a lovely angel-like figure, and she knew it was the old woman saying farewell.

Alice crept behind the last of the fairies. They soared up through a narrow tunnel. Around her were thick, dark stones, with a beam of light streaming in from above. But before Alice reached the top, she began to struggle. She turned to see that her wings were fading. She quickly caught hold of the stones, and began to haul herself up.

Now she understood what the old woman had meant. It was a terrible journey. The stones were rough, and soon her hands and feet were scratched and bleeding. The top of the tunnel seemed so far away, and she didn't dare look down. It felt as if she'd been climbing for days and days. But all the while, her ruby ring glowed bright, like a light in itself.

Then at last she was there! Back in the human world, in her own clothes once more.

"How beautiful it all is," she thought, gazing at the silvery trees and fields shining in the moonlight.

She didn't know which way to go, so she set off through the nearest field. Her hands and feet no longer hurt her.

"That must be because of my old woman," she was thinking, and then she saw, coming towards her, Aunt Judy.

"Alice! You've come back!"

Alice ran to her aunt. "Oh!" she said, hugging her. "I was afraid I'd been away for years. Are they all the same at home? Are you the same?"

"All is well, Alice. Come back home now. Your old friend told me all about your adventures."

"You know her too? Are you a sort of fairy? Is that why you're always happy?"

Aunt Judy shook her head, smiling. "When I was a little girl, she helped me. We've been lucky, you and I."

"Do they know – at home – what happened?"

"No. They wouldn't understand. But I think, perhaps, your mother knows there's something magical about the ring. That's why she gave it to you. She must have known you needed it."

As soon as they got back, Aunt Judy tucked Alice up in her bed.

"How will I feel in the morning?" asked Alice. "Will I be happy to be me again? Sometimes I don't like being myself. I'm not sure I'm brave enough to be just me…"

"Of course you'll be brave enough," said Aunt Judy. "You had the courage to try new things, to seek a new path, and to come back to those who love you. I know you will find the courage to do one of the hardest things of all – to learn to love yourself."

And when Alice woke in the morning, it was just as Aunt Judy said. She *did* feel happier, and her skin felt less prickly, and she couldn't wait to be with her family again.

Alice never spoke of the old woman, but she never forgot her. And whenever she looked at the ruby ring, she remembered her words… *Love your life and use it well, and have the courage to be yourself.*

About the Stories

The Prince in the Tower

A magical story, by Dinah Craik, about a prince imprisoned by his wicked uncle. The author started writing to earn money after her parents died, and was a strong believer in giving more opportunities to women, at a time when men had many more choices.

The Cuckoo Clock

This fantasy story is about a lonely girl, who learns about love and friendship. As a child, the author, Mary Molesworth, always loved to read and would listen to her Scottish grandmother, telling her epic tales from memory. Mary went on to write over 80 books for children.

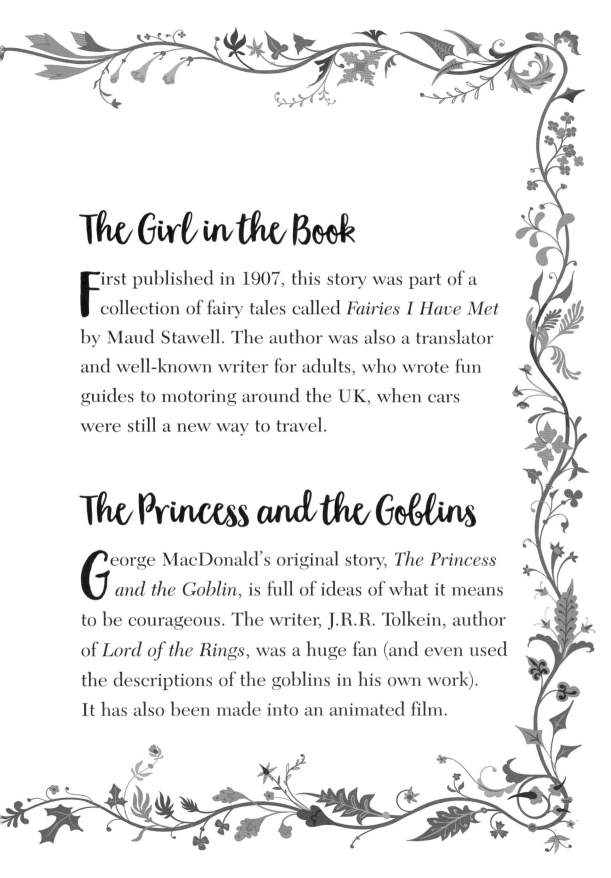

The Girl in the Book

First published in 1907, this story was part of a collection of fairy tales called *Fairies I Have Met* by Maud Stawell. The author was also a translator and well-known writer for adults, who wrote fun guides to motoring around the UK, when cars were still a new way to travel.

The Princess and the Goblins

George MacDonald's original story, *The Princess and the Goblin*, is full of ideas of what it means to be courageous. The writer, J.R.R. Tolkein, author of *Lord of the Rings*, was a huge fan (and even used the descriptions of the goblins in his own work). It has also been made into an animated film.

The Water Babies

Written by Charles Kingsley, *The Water Babies* was an instant hit when it was first published. In the story, Charles wanted to show how badly poor people in England were treated – and how shockingly hard life was for the children who were forced to go out to work.

Amelia and the Elves

This story was written by Juliana Ewing, who lived from 1841 to 1885, and was one of the best-selling children's authors of her day. Her books were described as the "first outstanding child-novels". She also edited *Aunt Judy's Magazine*, a hugely popular story magazine for children, set up by her mother.

The Ruby Ring

Mary Molesworth wrote *The Ruby Ring* in 1904, near the end of her long writing career. Like her other books, she wrote the story in a simple, straightforward style, so it would be easy for children to read, and – as in *The Cuckoo Clock* – she included elements of magic and fantasy. Although there is a strong moral, about appreciating what you have, Mary always wanted her books to be entertaining, rather than simply to teach a lesson.

Afterword from the Editors

Stories for children didn't always have magic and adventure in them. Around two hundred years ago, children's books were mostly very dull. Authors were more interested in teaching readers a moral, or a lesson, through their tales, than amusing them. But then, fairies and fantasy started to creep between the pages…

Writers such as Juliana Ewing, George MacDonald, Charles Kingsley, Diana Craik, Maud Stawell and Mary Molesworth began to tell tales for children that were full of flying cloaks, magic rings, goblins and fairy godmothers. They wove stories in dreamy underwater worlds, with butterfly balls, dancing elves, and birds that can fly you to the other side of the moon and back again.

These writers also wanted to inspire kindness and courage in their readers. In the stories we chose for this collection, the heroes learn to be kind to others, as well as how to be kind to themselves. They discover that true courage isn't just setting out on daring adventures, but also learning to stand up for yourself and for others.

Most of these stories are now well over a hundred years old. They – and their authors – have been largely forgotten. Their language, if you were to read the originals, might seem very old-fashioned, as would many of their ideas. But in re-telling them, we've kept the best parts: the magic, the adventure, and the message that all true heroes act with kindness and courage, and, in the end, strive to be their best selves.

Edited by Susanna Davidson
Designed by Samantha Barrett
Additional design by Tilly Kitching
Digital design: Nick Wakeford
Managing editor: Lesley Sims
Managing designer: Russell Punter

Disability expert: Lucy Catchpole

First published in 2021 by Usborne Publishing Ltd., Usborne House, 83-85 Saffron Hill, London EC1N 8RT, England. usborne.com Copyright © 2021 Usborne Publishing Ltd. UE. First published in America in 2021.